resurrected

(book #9 in the vampire journals)

morgan rice

ISBN: **978-1-939416-50-6**

"Who ever loved that loved not at first sight?"
—William Shakespeare

CHAPTER ONE

Caitlin sat in her living room, eyes raw from crying, exhausted, staring out at the blood-red sunset and hardly listening to the police officers who filled her room. She was in a daze. She slowly glanced about her room, and saw that it was filled with people—too many people.

Police officers, local cops, milled about her room, some sitting, others standing, several holding cups of coffee. They sat there with grim faces, lined up on the couches, in chairs, opposite her, asking endless questions. They had been here for hours. Everyone in this small town knew each other, and these were people who she had grown to know, who she had met at the supermarket, said hello to at local stores. She could hardly believe that they were here. In her house. It was like something out of a nightmare.

It was surreal. It had all happened so quickly, her life had turned upside down so easily, she could barely register it. She tried to grab hold of normal, of anything routine that used to give her comfort—but everything seemed to slip away. Normal didn't exist anymore.

Caitlin felt a reassuring hand squeeze hers and looked over and saw Caleb sitting beside her, his face pale with worry. On the overstuffed chairs beside them sat Sam and Polly, concern etched on their faces, too. This living room was crowded—way too crowded for Caitlin's taste. She wanted everyone in it to just disappear, everything to just go back to how it was the day before. Scarlet's sixteenth birthday, all of them sitting around the table, eating cake, laughing. Feeling as if all was perfect in the world, as if nothing would ever change.

Caitlin thought back to the night before, to her midnight thoughts, to her wishing her world, her life, was more than just mere normal. Now she regretted it. She would give anything to have normal back again.

It had been a whirlwind since she'd arrived home from her dreadful meeting with Aiden. After Scarlet had burst out the house,

Caitlin had ran after her, chased her down the side streets. Caleb had recovered from his blow, and had caught up with her, and the two of them had run through their little village, like mad people, trying to catch their daughter.

But it was no use. They were soon out of breath, Scarlet completely disappeared from view. She'd ran so fast, had leapt over an eight foot hedge in a single bound, without even slowing. Caleb had been amazed, although Caitlin had not: she knew what Scarlet was. She knew, even as she ran, that it was a futile effort, that Scarlet could run with lightning speed, leap over anything, and that within moments she would be completely lost, out of sight.

She was. They ran back to the house, jumped into their car, and had sped through the streets, frantically searching. But Caitlin knew, even as Caleb blew stop signs, took each turn hard, that they didn't stand a chance. They wouldn't catch her. Scarlet, she knew, was long gone.

After hours, finally, Caitlin had had enough, had insisted that they return home and call the police.

Now here they were, hours later, at almost midnight. Scarlet hadn't returned, and the police hadn't been able to find her. Luckily, it was a small town, with nothing else going on, and they had sent out cars immediately to search for her, and were still searching. The rest of the force—three officers seated across from them, along with the three officers standing around—remained here, asking question after question.

"Caitlin?"

Caitlin snapped out of it. She turned and saw the face of the officer seated on the couch across from her. Ed Hardy. He was a good man, had a daughter Scarlet's age, in her grade. He looked at her with sympathy and concern. She knew he felt her pain as a parent, and that he would do his best.

"I know this is hard," he said. "But we just have a few more questions. We really need to know everything if we're going to find Scarlet."

Caitlin nodded back. She tried to focus.

"I'm sorry," she said. "What else do you need to know?"

Officer Hardy cleared his throat, looking from Caitlin to Caleb, then back to her again. He seemed reluctant to proceed with his next question.

"I hate to ask this, but were there any arguments between you and your daughter in recent days?"

Caitlin looked back at him, puzzled.

"Arguments?" she asked.

"Any disagreements? Any fights? Any reason she would want to leave?"

Then Caitlin realized: he was asking her if Scarlet ran away. He still didn't understand.

She shook her head vehemently.

"There's no reason she'd want to leave. We never argued. Ever. We love Scarlet and Scarlet loves us. She's not the arguing type. She's not a rebel. She wouldn't run away. Don't you understand? That's not what this is about at all. Haven't you heard anything we've been telling you? She's sick! She needs help!"

Officer Hardy looked at his fellow officers, who looked back skeptically.

"I'm sorry to ask," he continued. "But you must realize, we get calls like this all the time. Teenage kids run away. That's what they do. They get mad at their parents. And in 99% of cases, they come back. Usually a few hours later. Sometimes a day or two. They crash at a friend's house. They just want to get away from their folks. And it's usually preceded by an argument."

"There was no argument," Caleb chimed in, forcefully. "Scarlet was as happy as can be. We celebrated her sixteenth birthday last night. Like Caitlin said, she's not that kind of girl."

"I feel like you're still not listening to a word we said," Caitlin added. "We told you, Scarlet was sick. She was sent home early from school. She was having…I don't know what. Convulsions…maybe seizures. She jumped out of bed and ran out the house. This isn't the case of a runaway. It's a child who is sick. Who needs medical attention."

Officer Hardy looked again at his fellow officers, who continued to look skeptical.

"I'm sorry, but what you're telling us just doesn't make any sense. If she was sick, how could she run out the house?"

"You said you chased her," chimed in another officer, edgier. "How could she have outrun you both? Especially if she was sick?"

Caleb shook his head, looking baffled himself.

"I don't know," he said. "But that's what happened."

"It's true. Every word of it is true," Caitlin said softly, remorsefully.

She was getting a sinking feeling that these men wouldn't understand. But she knew why Scarlet was able to outrun them; she knew why she was able to run when sick. She knew the answer—the one that would explain everything. But it was the one answer she could not give, the one that these men would never believe. They were not convulsions; they were hunger pangs. Scarlet was not running; she was hunting. And that was because her daughter was a vampire.

Caitlin flinched inside, burning to tell them, but knowing it was an answer that these men would be unable to hear. So instead, she stared solemnly out the window, hoping, praying, Scarlet would come back. That she might get better. That she hadn't fed. Hoping that these men would go away, leave her alone. She knew they were useless anyway. Calling them had been a mistake.

"I hate to say this," added the third officer, "but what you're describing…your daughter coming home from school, having seizures, having an adrenaline rush, bursting out the door…. I hate to say this, but it sounds like drugs. Maybe cocaine. Or Meth. It sounds like she was high on something. Like she had a bad trip. And adrenaline kicked in."

"You don't know what you're talking about," Caleb shot back at him. "Scarlet is not that kind of girl. She's never done drugs in her life."

The three officers looked at each other, skeptical.

"I know it's hard for you to hear," Officer Hardy said softly, "it's hard for most parents to hear. But our kids lead lives we never know about. You don't know what she's doing behind the scenes, with her friends."

"Did she bring around any new friends lately?" another officer asked.

Suddenly, Caleb's face hardened.

"Last night, actually," he said, anger rising in his voice. "She brought around a new boyfriend. Blake. They went to the movies together."

The three cops looked at each other with a knowing look.

"You think that's it?" Caleb asked. "Do you think this kid is pushing drugs on her?" As Caleb asked it, he started to sound more

10

sure of it himself, more optimistic that he'd found a neat answer to explain everything.

Caitlin sat there silently, just wanting this to end. She was burning to tell them all the real reason. But she knew it wouldn't do any good.

"What's his last name?" one of the officers asked.

"I have no idea." Caleb turned and looked at Caitlin. "Do you?"

Caitlin shook her head, and turned to Sam and Polly. "You guys?"

They shook their heads.

"Maybe I can find out," Polly said. "If they were friends on Facebook…" Polly began, then took out her cell phone and started typing. "I'm friends with Scarlet on Facebook. I don't know what her settings are, but maybe I can view her other friends. And if she's friends with him…."

Polly typed, and her eyes lit up.

"Here! Blake Robertson. Yeah, this is him!"

The cops leaned over and Polly reached out and held up her cell. They took it, handing it one to the other, looking closely at his face, writing down his last name.

"We'll talk to him," Officer Hardy said, as they handed Polly back her phone. "Maybe he knows something."

"What about Scarlet's other friends?" another officer asked. "Have you contacted them yet?"

Caitlin looked at Caleb blankly, realizing they'd been too dazed.

"I didn't think of it," Caitlin said. "It never occurred to me. She wasn't going to a friend's house. She was sick. It wasn't like she had a destination."

"Do it," an officer said. "Contact all of them. It's the best place to start."

"I have to say, from everything I'm hearing," Officer Hardy concluded, ready to wrap things up, "this sounds like drugs. I think Bob's right. Sounds like a bad trip. In the meantime, we'll keep patrolling the streets. The best thing you two can do is stay put. Wait for her here. She'll be back."

The officers looked at each other, then all at once they stood. Caitlin could see they were impatient to leave.

Caleb, Sam and Polly stood, and slowly, Caitlin stood, too, feeling weak in her knees. As she shook their hands, as they all prepared to leave, suddenly, something came over her. She couldn't remain silent

11

any longer. She could no longer contain the burning desire inside her to tell these people what she knew. To tell them that they weren't thinking about this the right way.

"What if it's something else?" Caitlin suddenly called out, as the cops were about to leave.

They all stopped, in the midst of putting on their coats, and slowly, they turned back to her.

"What do you mean?" Officer Hardy asked.

Caitlin, heart pounding in her chest, cleared her throat. She knew she shouldn't tell them; she would just seem crazy. But she couldn't hold it inside any longer.

"What if my daughter is possessed?" she asked.

They all stood there and stared back at her as if she were absolutely crazy.

"Possessed?" one of them asked.

"What if she's not herself anymore?" Caitlin asked. "What if she's changing? Into something else?"

A thick, heavy silence filled the room, and Caitlin felt everyone, including Caleb and Sam and Polly, turning and staring at her. Her cheeks flushed with embarrassment. But she couldn't stop. Not now. She had to plunge forward. And she knew, even as she did it, that this would be the turning point, the moment when the entire town no longer looked at her as a normal person, when her life here would change forever.

"What if my daughter is becoming a vampire?"

CHAPTER TWO

After Caleb had seen the policemen out, he closed the door and marched back into the room, scowling at Caitlin. She had never seen him look at her with such anger before, and her heart sank. She felt as if her whole life were unraveling before her eyes.

"You can't go speaking like that in public!" he snapped. "You sound like a crazy person! They're going to think we're all crazy. They're not going to take us seriously."

"I'm NOT crazy!" Caitlin snapped back. "And you should be taking my side, not theirs, and stop pretending like everything is normal. You were in that room with me. You know what you saw. Scarlet threw you across the room. Would a seizure cause that? A sickness?"

"So what are you saying?" Caleb retorted, his voice rising. "That means she's a monster? A vampire? That's ridiculous. You sound as if you're losing touch with reality."

Caitlin's voice rose right back at him. "Then how do you explain it?"

"There are a lot of explanations," he said.

"Like what?"

"Maybe it has something to do with her sickness. Or maybe, like they said, she was on some kind of drug. Maybe that kid Blake—"

"That's ridiculous," Caitlin spat. "Blake is a good kid. He's not a drug pusher. And besides, you saw how she outran us. We didn't even stand a chance. That wasn't normal. Don't pretend you didn't see what you did."

"I'm not going to listen to any more of this," Caleb said.

He turned and marched across the room, yanked his army coat off the hook, put it on and quickly zipped it up.

"Where are you going?" Caitlin asked.

"I'm going to find her. I can't just sit here. It's driving me crazy. I have to look."

"The cops said the best place to be is here. What if she comes home while you're out there?" Caitlin asked.

13

"Then you can stay here and call me," Caleb snapped. "I'm going out."

With that, he crossed the room, opened the door, and slammed it behind him. Caitlin listened to the sound of his boots quickly descending the porch steps, crunching across the gravel, then heard him get into their car and take off.

Caitlin felt like crying. She didn't want to fight with Caleb—especially now. But she couldn't let him convince her she was losing touch with reality. She knew what she saw. And she knew that she was right. She wasn't going to let others convince her she was losing her mind.

Caitlin turned to Sam and Polly, who stood there, very still, eyes opened wide in surprise. They had never seen Caitlin and Caleb fight before. Caitlin herself had never seen them fight before—up until this moment, their relationship had never been anything but harmonious. Sam and Polly both looked stunned, afraid to interfere. They also looked at her as if she were a bit crazy, not in her right mind. She wondered if maybe they sided with Caleb.

"I feel like maybe I should be out there searching, too," Sam said tentatively. "Two cars searching the streets is better than one. And I'm pretty useless in here. Is that okay?" he asked Caitlin.

Caitlin nodded back, afraid to open her mouth for fear she would cry. Sam was right; he wouldn't be much use here in the house. And she had Polly. Sam came over and gave her a quick hug, then turned and left.

"I'll be on my cell," he said, as he left. "Call me if you hear anything."

Sam closed the door behind him and Polly came over to Caitlin and gave her a long hug. Caitlin hugged her back. It felt so good to have her best friend here, by her side. She didn't know what she would do without her.

The two of them sat side-by-side on the couch, as Caitlin wiped away a tear forming at the corner of her eyes. Her eyes were already red and raw from all the hours of crying. Now, she just felt hollowed out.

"I'm so so so sorry," Polly said. "This is a nightmare. Just awful. There are no words. I don't understand what happened. None of it makes any sense. I know that Scarlet didn't do drugs. She wouldn't. And you're right: Blake seems like a good kid."

14

Caitlin sat there, looking out the window at the falling night, and nodded blankly. She wanted to talk, but she felt so shaky, she was afraid she would burst into tears again if she did.

"What do you think about what the police said?" Polly asked. "About contacting her friends? Do you think that's a good idea?"

As Polly said it, Caitlin suddenly remembered it, and realized it was the perfect thing to do. She racked her brain, wondering how to get in touch with her friends.

Then it hit her: Scarlet's phone. She'd burst out of here without even pausing to grab it. Her phone must be somewhere in the house. Maybe in her bag. Probably in her bedroom.

Caitlin jumped up from the couch.

"You're right," she said. "Her phone. It must be in her bedroom."

Caitlin ran across the room and up the steps, Polly and Ruth on her heels.

She hurried into Scarlet's bedroom, saw the upturned sheets and pillows, saw the dent in the sheetrock where Caleb had been thrown, where her own head had hit, and remembered. It brought it all back, and made her feel queasy as she relived it again. It looked like the scene of a disaster.

Caitlin felt a surge of determination as she scoured the room. She rifled through the mess on her desk, on her dresser—then spotted her bag, hanging on a chair. She rummaged through it, feeling a bit guilty, and felt for her phone. She pulled it out, victorious.

"You found it!" Polly yelled, hurrying over.

Caitlin saw there was still some battery life. She opened it, feeling bad for spying, but knowing that she needed to. She didn't know Scarlet's friends numbers, and had no other way of getting in touch with them.

She tapped on Scarlet's contacts, then went to her Favorites. She scrolled through, and saw dozens of names. Some names she recognized, and others she didn't.

"We should call them all," Polly said. "One by one. Maybe one of them knows something."

Caitlin stood there, in a daze, suddenly feeling overwhelmed. As she went to dial the first contact, she noticed how badly her hands were shaking.

Polly noticed, too; she reached out and placed a reassuring hand on Caitlin's wrist, and Caitlin looked up.

"Caitlin, sweety, you're still in shock. Let me call all these people for you. Please. It would give me something to do. Just go and sit down and rest. You've been through hell, and you've already done all that you can."

As Polly said it, Caitlin knew she was right. She wasn't really in her right mind. She looked at the phone, and for a moment, almost forgot what she was doing. She reached out and handed the phone to Polly.

Caitlin turned and walked out the room, and within moments, she heard Polly's voice ringing through the air, already having someone on the line.

"Is this Heather?" Polly called out. "This is Polly Paine. I'm Scarlet Paine's aunt. I'm sorry to trouble you, but we're looking for Scarlet. Have you seen her?"

Polly's voice slowly faded as Caitlin walked back down the steps. She held the banister as she went, feeling dizzy, feeling as if the world might slip out from under her.

She finally entered the living room, walked over to a large, overstuffed chair, and sank into it. She sat there, staring out the window, her mind racing. Despite her best efforts, images flashed through her mind: Scarlet in bed, screaming; her snarl; her throwing Caleb; her bursting out of the house…. Was it all real?

As she dwelled on it, she couldn't help thinking of her meeting with Aiden. Of his words, of her journal. Had her journal caused all this? Why had she had to go to that stupid attic? Why did she have to go visit him? If she hadn't, if she'd left everything alone, would all of this had happened?

She thought of Aiden's warning, that Scarlet would unleash vampirism back onto the world.

You must stop her.

Caitlin sat there, wondering. What was Scarlet out there doing right now? Was she feeding on people? Was she turning them into vampires? Was she spreading it, even now? Would the world never be the same? Was Caitlin responsible?

Caitlin felt like grabbing her phone and calling Aiden. Grilling him. Demanding he tell her everything, every last detail.

16

But she couldn't bring herself to. She reached out and held her phone, and something inside her stopped. She remembered Aiden's final words, and they brought a fresh wave of nausea. She loved Scarlet more than life, and could never entertain harming her.

As Caitlin sat there, clutching the phone, staring out the window, hearing Polly's muted voice from upstairs, her mind raced. Her eyelids grow heavy. Before she knew it, she was fast asleep.

*

Caitlin woke to find herself sitting alone in her large, empty house. The world was still. She sat there, wondering where everyone had gone, and stood and crossed the room. Oddly, all the blinds and drapes had been drawn tight. She walked to one of the windows, and pulled them back. As she looked out, she saw a blood-red sun—but this time it looked different. It didn't seem like sunset, but rather sunrise. She was confused. Had she slept the whole night? Had Scarlet come home? And where had everyone gone?

Caitlin headed towards the front door. For some reason she sensed that maybe Scarlet was there, waiting for her.

She slowly pulled open the heavy door, looking out. But the world was absolutely still. There wasn't a single person on the streets, or even a single car in sight. All she could hear was the sound of a lone morning bird chirping. She looked up and saw it was a raven.

Caitlin heard a sudden noise, and turned and walked back through the house. She walked into the kitchen, looking for signs of anyone. She heard another clanging, and made her way to the window against the back wall. The drapes were drawn tightly here, too, which was odd, because Caitlin always kept them open. She reached for the drapes, and pulled the cord.

As she did, she jumped back in fright. Standing outside, its face to the window, was the pale, white face of a vampire, completely bald, fangs extended and right up against the glass. It snarled and hissed as it reached up with its hands and placed its palms against the glass. Caitlin could see its long, yellow fingernails.

There was another sudden noise, and Caitlin turned and saw the face of another vampire at the side window.

There was the sound of breaking glass, and she turned and in the other direction saw yet another face. This one smashed his head right to the glass, sneering at her.

Suddenly, her house was filled with the sound of breaking glass. Caitlin ran through the house, and everywhere she looked, the walls were different than she remembered. Now they were all made of glass windows, and everywhere she looked, drapes were being pulled back and windows shattered, as vampire after vampire stuck its head through.

Caitlin ran from room to room, to the front door, trying to get away, as more and more windows shattered.

She reached the front door and yanked it open—and stopped in her tracks.

Standing there, facing her, a deadly look in her eyes, was Scarlet. She glared back at Caitlin, looking more dead than alive, stark white, and with a fierce look that wanted to kill. Even more shocking, behind her stood an army of vampires—thousands of them. All waiting to follow her, to rush into Caitlin's house.

"Scarlet?" she asked, hearing the fear in her own voice.

But before she could react, Scarlet grimaced, leaned back, and pounced on Caitlin, her fangs aiming right for her throat.

Caitlin woke screaming, sitting up in her chair. She reached for her throat, rubbing it with one hand, while with her other hand, she tried to push Scarlet off.

"Caitlin? You OK?"

After several seconds, Caitlin calmed down and looked up and realized it wasn't Scarlet. It was Sam. At first, she was confused. Then she realized, with tremendous relief, that she had been sleeping. It was just a nightmare.

Caitlin sat there, breathing hard. Standing over her were Sam, one hand on her shoulder, looking concerned, and Polly. The lamps were on, and she saw it was dark out. She glanced at the grandfather clock and saw it was after midnight. She must have fallen asleep in the chair.

"You okay?" Sam asked again.

Now Caitlin was embarrassed. She sat up, wiping her forehead.

"Sorry to wake you, but it seemed like you were having a bad dream," Polly added.

Caitlin slowly stood, pacing, trying to shake off the awful vision of the dream. It had felt so real, she could almost still feel the pain in her throat where she had been bitten by her own daughter.

But it was just a dream. She had to keep telling herself that. Just a dream.

"Where's Caleb?" she asked, remembering. "Have you heard anything? How did the calls go?"

The expressions on Sam's and Polly's faces told her all she needed to know.

"Caleb's still out there looking," Sam said. "I called it quits about an hour ago. It's pretty late. But we wanted to keep you company until he got home."

"I called all her friends," Polly chimed in. "Every single one. I got through to most of them. No one has seen or heard anything. They were all as surprised as we were. I even got through to Blake. But he said he hasn't heard a word from her. I'm so sorry."

Caitlin rubbed her face, trying to shake off the cobwebs. She had hoped to wake to find that none of this was real. That Scarlet was back, home, safe. That life had gone back to normal. But seeing Sam and Polly standing there, in her house, after midnight, looking so concerned, brought it all back. It was all real. Too real. Scarlet was missing. And might not ever come back.

The realization struck Caitlin like a knife. She could barely breathe at the thought of it. Scarlet, her only daughter. The person she loved most in life. She couldn't possibly imagine life without her. She wanted to run out there, down every street, to scream and yell at the unfairness of it all. But she knew it would be useless. She just had to sit here, and wait.

Suddenly, there was a noise at the door. The three of them jumped up and looked, hoping. Caitlin ran to it, praying to see the familiar face of her teenage daughter.

But her heart fell to see it was just Caleb. Returning home—and with a grim expression on his face. The sight of it made her heart drop further. He had clearly been unsuccessful.

She knew it was useless, but she asked anyway: "Anything?"

Caleb looked to the floor as he shook his head. He looked like a broken man.

Sam and Polly exchanged a look, then came over to Caitlin and each gave her a hug.

19

"I'll be back first thing in the morning," Caitlin said. "Call me if you hear anything. Even if it's the middle of the night. Promise?"

Caitlin nodded back, too overwhelmed to speak. She felt Polly hug her, and hugged her back, then hugged her little brother.

"I love you, sis," he said over her shoulder. "Hang in there. She'll be okay."

Caitlin wiped away tears and watched Sam and Polly walk out the door.

Now, it was just her and Caleb. Usually, she'd be thrilled to be alone with him—but after their fight, she felt nervous. Caleb, she could see, was lost in his own world of misery and regret; she also sensed he was still mad at her for voicing her theories to the police.

It was all too much for Caitlin to bear. She realized she'd been holding out hope for Caleb's return, a shred of optimism that he would waltz in and announce something, some good news. But to see him returning like this, with nothing, nothing at all, just brought it all home for her. Scarlet had been gone all day. Nobody knew where she was. It was after midnight and she hadn't come home. She knew what a bad sign that was. She didn't even want to entertain the possibilities, but she knew it was very, very bad.

"I'm going to bed," Caleb announced, as he turned and strutted up the steps.

Caleb always said "good night," always asked her to come to bed with him. In fact, Caitlin could not remember a night they had not gone to bed together.

Now, he didn't even ask.

Caitlin went back to her chair in the living room, and sat there, listening to his boots climb the steps, hearing their bedroom door close behind him. It was the loneliest sound she'd ever heard.

She burst into tears, and she cried for she didn't know how long. Eventually she curled up into a ball, crying into the pillow. She vaguely remembered Ruth coming up to her, trying to lick her face; but it was all just a blur, because soon, her body racked with sobs, she fell into a deep and fitful sleep.

CHAPTER THREE

Caitlin felt something cold and wet on her face, and slowly opened her eyes. Disoriented, she was looking at her living room, sideways; she realized she had fallen asleep on the chair. The room was dim, and from the muted light coming through the drapes, she realized day was just beginning to break. The sound of pouring rain slammed against the glass.

Caitlin heard whining, and felt something wet on her face again and looked over and saw Ruth, standing over her, licking her, whining hysterically. She was prodding her with her cold, wet snout, and she wouldn't quit.

Finally Caitlin sat up, realizing something was wrong. Ruth wouldn't stop whining, louder and louder, then finally barking at her—she'd never known her to act this way.

"What is it, Ruth?" Caitlin asked.

Ruth barked again, then turned and ran from the room, towards the front door. Caitlin looked down and in the dim light made out a trail of muddy pawprints all over the carpet. Ruth must have been outside, Caitlin realized. The front door must be open.

Caitlin hurried to her feet, realizing that Ruth was trying to tell her something, to lead her somewhere.

Scarlet, she thought.

Ruth barked again, and Caitlin felt that was it. Ruth was trying to lead her to Scarlet.

Caitlin ran out the room, her heart pounding. She didn't want to waste a second by running upstairs to get Caleb. She tore through the living room, through the parlor, and out the front door. *Where could Ruth have possibly found Scarlet?* she wondered. *Was she safe? Was she alive?*

Caitlin flooded with panic as she burst out the front door, already ajar from Ruth, who had somehow managed to get it open, and out onto the front porch. The world was filled with the sound of pouring rain. There was a soft, rumbling thunder, and a flash of lightning in the breaking dawn, and in the soft gray light, the torrential rain slammed down to earth.

Caitlin stopped at the top of the steps, as she saw where Ruth had went. She flooded with panic. Lightning filled the sky, and there, before her, was an image that traumatized her—one that lodged in her brain, one that she would never forget as long as she lived.

There, lying on the front lawn, curled up in a ball, unconscious, naked, was her daughter. Scarlet. Exposed to the rain.

Pacing over her, barking like crazy, Ruth looked back and forth between Caitlin and Scarlet.

Caitlin burst into action: she ran down the steps, tripping over them as she went, screaming out in terror as she ran for her daughter. Her mind raced with a million scenarios of what might have happened to her, where she might have went, how she might have returned. Whether she was healthy. Alive.

The worst possible scenarios all flashed through her mind at once, as Caitlin ran in the muddy grass, slipping and sliding.

"SCARLET!" Caitlin shrieked, and another clap of thunder met her cry.

It was the wail of a mother beside herself with grief, the wail of a mother who could not stop whaling as she ran to Scarlet, knelt beside her, scooped her up in her arms, and prayed to God with everything she had that her daughter was still alive.

CHAPTER FOUR

Caitlin sat beside Caleb in the stark-white hospital room, watching Scarlet sleep. The two of them sat in separate chairs, a few feet away from one another, each lost in their own world. They were both so emotionally drained, so panic-stricken, they hadn't any energy left to even speak to each other. In all the other tough times in their marriage, they'd always found solace in each other; but this time was different. The incidents of the last day had been too dramatic, too terrifying. Caitlin was still in shock; so, she knew, was Caleb. They each needed to process it their own way.

They sat there in silence, watching Scarlet sleep, the only sound in the room the beeping of the various machines. Caitlin was afraid to take her eyes off her daughter, afraid that if she looked away, she might lose her again. The clock over Scarlet's head read 8 AM, and Caitlin realized she'd been sitting there for the last three hours, ever since they'd admitted her, watching. Scarlet had not awakened since they'd brought her in.

The nurses had reassured them several times that all of Scarlet's vitals were normal, that she was just in a deep sleep, and that there was nothing to worry about. On the one hand, Caitlin was greatly relieved; but on the other, she wouldn't really believe it until she saw for herself, saw Scarlet awake, her eyes open, saw the same old Scarlet she had always known—happy and healthy.

Caitlin ran through in her mind, again and again, the events of the past 24 hours. But no matter how she dissected them, none of it made any sense—unless she returned to the same conclusion: that Aiden was right. Her journal was real. That her daughter was a vampire. That she, Caitlin, once had been one, too. That she had traveled back in time, had found the antidote, and had chosen to return here, to this time and place, to live out a normal life. The Scarlet was the last remaining vampire on earth.

The thought terrified Caitlin. She was so protective of Scarlet and determined that nothing bad should happen to her; yet, at the same time, she also felt a responsibility to humanity, felt that if all this were true, she could not allow Scarlet to spread it, to re-create the vampire race once again. She hardly knew what to do, and she didn't know what to think, or to believe. Her own husband didn't believe her, and she could hardly blame him. She hardly believed herself.

"Mom?"

Caitlin sat upright as she saw Scarlet's eyes flutter open. She jumped up from her chair, and ran over to her bedside, as did Caleb. The two hovered over Scarlet as she slowly opened her big, beautiful eyes, lit up by the morning sun coming through the window.

"Scarlet? Honey?" Caitlin asked. "Are you okay?"

Scarlet yawned and rubbed her eyes with the back of her hands, then slowly rolled over onto her back, blinking, disoriented.

"Where am I?" she asked.

Caitlin was flooded with relief at the sound of her voice; she sounded, and looked, like the same old Scarlet. There was strength in her voice, strength in her movements, in her facial expressions. In fact, to Caitlin's utter surprise, Scarlet looked completely normal, as if she'd just casually awakened from a long sleep.

"Scarlet, do you remember anything that happened?" Caitlin asked.

Scarlet turned and looked at her, then slowly propped herself up on one elbow, sitting up partially.

"Am I in a hospital?" she asked, surprised. She surveyed the room, realizing she was. "OMG. What am I doing here? Did I get really sick?"

Caitlin felt an even greater sense of relief at her words—and her motions. She was sitting up. She was alert. Her voice was completely normal. Her eyes were bright. It was hard to believe that anything abnormal had ever happened.

Caitlin thought about how to respond, how much to tell her. She didn't want to scare her.

"Yes honey," Caleb interjected. "You were sick. The nurse sent you home from school, and we took you to the hospital this morning. Do you remember any of it?"

"I remember being sent home from school…being in bed, in my room…then…" She furrowed her brow, as if trying to remember. "…that's about it. What was it? A fever? Whatever. I feel fine now."

Caleb and Caitlin both exchanged a confused look. Clearly, Scarlet seemed normal, and didn't remember anything.

Should we tell her? Caitlin wondered.

She didn't want to terrify her. But at the same time, she felt that she needed to know, needed to know some part of what happened to her. She could sense Caleb was thinking the same thing.

"Scarlet, honey," Caitlin began softly, trying to think how to best phrase her words, "when you were sick, you jumped out of bed and ran out the house. Do you remember that?"

Scarlet looked at her, eyes widening in surprise.

"Really?" she asked. "Ran out the house? What do you mean? Like, sleepwalking? How far did I go?"

Caitlin and Caleb exchanged a look.

"You actually ran pretty far," Caitlin said. "We couldn't find you for a while. We called the police, and we called some of your friends—"

"Seriously?" Scarlet asked, sitting upright, reddening. "You called my friends? Why? That's so embarrassing. How did you get their numbers?" Then she realized. "Did you raid my phone? How could you do that?"

She leaned back in bed, sighing, staring at the ceiling, exasperated.

"This is so mortifying. I'll never live this down. How am I going to face everyone? Now they'll think I'm some kind of freak or something."

"Honey, I'm sorry, but you were sick, and we couldn't find you—"

Suddenly the door to the room opened, and in walked a man who was clearly her doctor, strutting in with authority, flanked by two residents, each holding clipboards. They walked right to the clipboard at the base of Scarlet's bed and read the chart.

Caitlin was glad for the interruption, defusing their argument.

A nurse trailed them, and walked up to Scarlet and raised her hospital bed to a sitting position. She wrapped her bicep and read her blood pressure, then inserted a digital thermostat in her ear and read it to the doctor.

"Normal," she announced to the doctor, as he read the clipboard, nodding. "The same as when she came in here. We found nothing wrong with her at all."

"I feel fine," Scarlet chimed in. "I know I was sick yesterday, I guess I had a fever or whatever. But I'm fine now. Actually, I'd really like to go to school. I have a lot of tests today. And some damage control to do," she added, looking angrily at her parents. "And I'm hungry. Can I go now?"

Caitlin was worried by Scarlet's reaction, her insistence on trying to just brush all this under the rug and jump back into normal life. She looked at Caleb, hoping he felt the same, but she sensed in him, too, a desire to forget all this and to rush back to normalcy. He seemed relieved.

"Scarlet," the doctor began. "Is it okay if I examine you and ask you a few questions?"

"Sure."

He handed his clipboard to one of his residents, removed his stethoscope, placed it on her chest, and listened. He then placed his fingers on various spots on her stomach, then reached out and took her wrists, and bent her arms in various directions. He felt her lymph nodes, felt her throat, and felt the pressure points behind her elbows and knees.

"I'm told you were sent home from school yesterday with a fever," he said. "How do you feel now?"

"I feel great," she responded, chipper.

"Can you describe to me how you were feeling yesterday?" he pressed.

Scarlet furrowed her brow.

"It's kind of hazy, to be honest," she said. "I was in class and I, like, started to feel really sick. My head hurt, and the light hurt my eyes, and I felt really achy…I remember feeling really cold when I got home….But other than that it's kind of a blur."

"Do you have any memory of yesterday, of anything that happened after you got sick?" he asked.

"I was just telling my parents, I don't. I'm sorry. They said I was like sleepwalking or something. But I don't remember. Anyway, I'd really like to get back to class."

The doctor smiled.

"You're a strong and brave young girl, Scarlet. I admire your work ethic. I wish that all teenagers were like you," he said with a wink. "If you don't mind, I'd like to talk to your parents for a few minutes. And yes, I see no reason why you can't return to school. I'll talk to the nurses and we'll begin the paperwork to discharge you."

"Yes!" Scarlet said, clenching her first in excitement as she sat up, her eyes gleaming.

The doctor turned to Caitlin and Caleb.
"May I talk to the two of you in private?"

CHAPTER FIVE

Caitlin and Caleb follow the doctor down the hall and into his large, brightly-lit office, the morning sun streaming in through the windows.

"Please, take a seat," he said in his reassuring, authoritative voice, gesturing towards the two chairs opposite his desk, as he closed the door behind them.

Caitlin and Caleb sat and the doctor walked around his desk, holding his file, and took a seat behind his desk. He adjusted his glasses on the bridge of his nose, glancing down at some notes, then removed his glasses, closed the folder, and pushed it to the side of his desk. He folded his hands and rested them on his stomach, leaning back slightly in his chair as he studied them both. Caitlin felt reassured in his presence, and sensed he was good at what he did. She also liked how kind he had been to Scarlet.

"Your daughter is fine," he began. "She's absolutely normal. Her vitals are normal, and have been normal since she arrived, and she shows no sign of having had any convulsions or seizures or any epileptic disorders. She also shows no signs of neurological problems. Given the fact that you found her unclothed, we also checked for any signs of sexual activity—and there were none whatsoever. We also ran a slew of blood tests on her, all of which have come back negative. You can set your mind at ease: there is absolutely nothing wrong with your daughter."

Caleb sighed in relief.

"Thank you, doctor," he said. "You don't know what that means to us to hear that."

But inside, Caitlin was still shaking. She didn't feel a sense of peace yet. If the doctor had told her that, in fact, Scarlet was positive for a medical condition, she would have, paradoxically, felt much better, more of a sense of ease: at least then she would know exactly what was wrong with her, and could discount any thoughts of vampirism.

But hearing this, that there was nothing medically wrong with her, only deepened Caitlin's sense of dread.

"So then how do you explain what happened?" Caitlin asked the doctor, her voice trembling.

He turned and looked at her.

"Please tell me: what exactly *did* happen?" he asked. "I only know what the file says: that she had a fever yesterday afternoon, was sent home from school, that she ran out of the house, and that you found her on your lawn this morning. Is that accurate?"

"There's more to it than that," Caitlin snapped, determined to be heard. "She didn't just run of the house. She..." Caitlin paused, trying to figure out how to phrase it. "She...transformed. Her level of strength—it's hard to explain. My husband tried to stop her, and she threw him across the room. She threw me across the room, too. And her speed: we chased after her, and couldn't catch her. It was no normal 'running out of the house.' Something happened to her. Something physical."

The doctor sighed.

"I realize this must have been very scary for you," he said, "as it would be for any parent. But I can assure you again that there is nothing wrong with her. We encounter episodes like this from time to time, especially amongst teenagers. In fact, there is an age-old diagnosis for it: Conversion Syndrome. Formerly known as 'hysteria.' Fits like this can overwhelm the patient, and they can experience a surge of strength, and do things out of character. The state can last for several hours, after which they often return to normal. It is especially prevalent amongst teenage girls. No one knows its exact cause, although generally, it is brought on by a stressor. Did Scarlet experience any stress in the days leading up to the event? Anything different? Anything at all?"

Caitlin slowly shook her head, still not buying it.

"Everything was perfect in her life. The night before was her sixteenth birthday. She introduced us to her new boyfriend. She was as happy as can be. She had no stress whatsoever."

The doctor smiled back.

"That is, she had no stress that you could see—or that she chose to reveal to you. But I think you've answered your own question: you said that she introduced you to her new boyfriend. Don't you think that could be stressful in the eyes of a teenage girl? Parental approval?

That certainly could have surfaced any latent stressors. Not to mention, her turning 16. High school, peer pressure, exams, SATs on the horizon…. There are an endless number of potential stressors there. Sometimes we don't always know what sets it off. Scarlet may not even know herself. But the important thing is, there is nothing to worry about here."

"Doctor," Caitlin continued, more firmly, "this wasn't merely a fit of hysteria, or whatever it is you're calling it. I'm telling you, something happened in that room. Something…supernatural."

The doctor looked long and hard at her, his eyes widening.

Caleb interjected, leaning forward.

"I'm sorry, doctor—my wife has been under a lot of stress lately, as you can understand."

"I'm *not* under stress," Caitlin snapped back, sounding way too stressed and contradicting her own words. "I know what I saw. Doctor, I need you to help her daughter. She is not normal. Something happened to her. She is changing. Please. There must be something you can do. Someplace we can bring her."

The doctor stared at Caitlin, looking stunned, for at least ten seconds. A thick silence hung in the air.

"Mrs. Paine," he began slowly, "with all due respect, I work in the medical profession. And medically, there is absolutely nothing wrong with your daughter. In fact, I heartily recommend that she go back to school today, and put this whole incident behind her as soon as she can. And as far as your…ideas…I don't mean to be patronizing, but may I ask: are you currently seeing anyone?"

Caitlin looked back at him blankly, trying to understand what he meant.

"Are you currently in therapy, Mrs. Paine?"

Caitlin blushed, finally realizing what he was saying. He thought she was crazy.

"No," she answered flatly.

He slowly nodded.

"Well, I realize today is about your daughter, not about you. But when things settle down, if I may, I do suggest that you talk to someone. It can help."

He reached out, grabbed a pad, and started scribbling.

"I'm giving you the name of a top-notch psychiatrist. Dr. Halsted, a colleague of mine. Please, use it. We all go through stressful times in life. He can help."

With that, the doctor suddenly stood, holding out the paper to Caitlin. She and Caleb stood, too, but as she stood there, looking out at the paper, she couldn't get herself to take it. She wasn't crazy. She knew what she saw.

And she wasn't going to accept the paper.

The doctor held the paper out there, awkwardly, his hand trembling, for way too long, until finally, Caleb reached out and took it from him.

"Thank you, doctor. And thank you for helping her daughter."

CHAPTER SIX

Caitlin and Caleb walked down the hospital corridor together, to the waiting area. Scarlet needed a few minutes to gather her things and get dressed, and they wanted to give her privacy. Caitlin could not believe how fast she was checking out: they would be out of their before 9 AM. Caitlin really wanted her to stay home and rest, but Scarlet insisted on going to school for the day.

It all felt surreal. Just hours ago Caitlin had been awakened by Ruth, wondering if her daughter was dead or alive. Now, by 9 AM, she was seemingly fine, and heading off to school. Caitlin knew she should be thrilled for the return to normalcy. But nothing felt normal to her anymore. Inside, she was trembling, sensing that far worse things could be coming down the road.

As they walked into the hospital atrium, a large, glass waiting room with soaring ceilings, huge shoots of bamboo, sunlight pouring through the glass and a large bubbling fountain in its center, Caleb seemed as happy as can be. She could sense he was determined to put all this behind them, to insist on things going back to normal. And that bothered her. It was like he was pretending that nothing unusual had happened.

"So is that it then?" she finally asked, as they crossed the huge, empty room, their footsteps echoing on the marble floor. "We just drop Scarlet off at school and pretend nothing ever happened?"

Caitlin didn't want to start a fight, but she couldn't help it. She couldn't just let this go.

"What else are we supposed to do?" he asked. "She said she's fine. The doctor said she's fine. The nurses say she's fine. All the tests show that she's fine. She doesn't want to go back home. And I don't blame her. Why should she sit alone in her room all day, lying in bed, when she wants to go to school?

"And frankly," he added, "I think it's a good idea. I think she should get on with her life. I think we *all* should," he added, looking at Caitlin strangely, as if giving her a message. "It was a terrible day and night, not knowing where she was, or what really even happened. But

32

she's back to us. That's all that matters. That's all I care about. I want to put this behind us, and move forward. I don't want to dwell on it. I don't think it's helpful for Scarlet to, either. I don't want her to get some kind complex, to start worrying about herself, if she's normal. I'm just so grateful that she's back to us, and that she's safe and healthy. That's all that matters, isn't it?"

As he stopped and turned to her, the morning light lit up his large brown eyes; in them, Caitlin saw hope, desperation, and a pleading for her to say that everything was fine again, that they would put it all behind them.

More than anything, Caitlin wanted to. As she looked into those eyes, she just wanted them to be happy. She really didn't want to argue. But as much as she wanted to just shove this under the rug, she couldn't. Her daughter's life, her health—her future—was at stake. And so was the future of mankind. As unpleasant as it might be, she felt she had to get to the bottom of it.

"I don't think she should be rushing back to school so quickly, regardless of what she says, or the doctor says," Caitlin said, hearing the determination in her own voice as she tried to stay calm. "I think she needs further testing. This doctor is a part of the establishment. Maybe she needs to see an alternative doctor. A specialist."

"What kind of specialist?" Caleb snapped back. "What kind of testing?"

Caitlin shrugged. She wished she knew. She wished there was someone who could give her the answers she wanted, someone who could prove to her that she wasn't crazy. As Caleb looked at her, she could see in his eyes that he, too, thought she was losing it.

"I don't know, exactly," Caitlin said. "I'm not an expert. But there might be people who are."

"An expert in what?" he pressed, impatient.

Caitlin was beginning to feel upset as she looked back at him.

"How can you just stand there and pretend that nothing happened in that room? You can tell the cops, and the doctor, whatever you want, but between you and me, between the two of us, you know what happened. You know what you saw."

Caleb turned from her, impatient.

"I don't know what you're talking about," he said.

"Oh yes you do," Caitlin said. "You saw what happened to our daughter. You heard her snarl. She threw you across the room—and there's still a dent to prove it!"

"So what!?" he snapped, at the end of his rope.

"How do you explain it?"

"You heard the doctor. Conversion syndrome. People get into altered states. They can do anything. It's like a fit of hysteria, like he said. You hear stories of adrenaline rushes, of what people can do. It doesn't mean anything. It doesn't prove anything."

"That was no adrenaline rush! And that was not Conversion Syndrome!" Caitlin shot back, his voice rising.

"She had a high fever. She was in an altered state. It was like a form of sleepwalking," he pleaded.

"That was *not* sleepwalking!"

"It doesn't matter what you call it. Why harp on it? There is *nothing* wrong with our daughter!" Caleb yelled back, his voice rising several levels. His voice echoed in the big empty chamber, and the few people standing on the periphery turned their way.

Caitlin saw them looking, as did Caleb, and they both turned and looked away, embarrassed.

"I wish I could believe that," Caitlin said, softly. "I really do. She might be okay for now. But she's not okay. She needs help. And I'm going to find it for her. No matter what you say, or what she says."

"Help for what?" Caleb retorted. "What exactly is it that you think she needs help from?"

"You know what it is. You know what I said. You can choose not to believe it, but you know it's true."

She saw hesitation in Caleb's eyes size, but still, he pressed the question

"*What* is true?"

Finally, Caitlin lost it.

"OUR DAUGHTER IS A VAMPIRE!"

Caitlin's shout rose to the glass ceiling, echoed throughout the room—and every person turned and stared.

Caleb turned and looked at them all, then lowered his head, embarrassed. Finally, he stepped up, and looked at Caitlin, right in the eyes. She stood there, shaking, rooted to the spot, not knowing what to do, how to feel.

Slowly, disapprovingly, he shook his head.

"The doctor was right," he said. "You do need help."

*

Caitlin, in a daze, drove slowly, Scarlet in the passenger seat, as she took her to school. Caleb had left for work, leaving Caitlin to drop her off, and she and Scarlet had been driving in silence for the last few minutes, as Caitlin watched the road, trying to process it all, while Scarlet sat in the front seat, glued to her phone, texting with several of her friends.

"Major damage control, mom," she said. "I so wish you hadn't called all my friends," she sighed.

Caitlin didn't know how to respond.

Scarlet checked her phone again. "I can still make second period," she said. "That's perfect. I don't have my first test until fourth. I'm staying late today, don't forget—soccer," she said in a rush, as Caitlin pulled up before the main doors of the school.

Scarlet leaned over and kissed Caitlin on the cheek, as she opened the door. "Don't worry about me. I'm fine. Really. Whatever it was, it was no big deal. Love you," she said in a rush, jumping out before Caitlin could respond and rushing up the steps to the front doors of the school.

Caitlin watched her go with a sinking feeling in her chest. She felt so sad, so helpless, so terrified. There went Scarlet, her only daughter, the person she loved most in the world. She wanted to protect her. And to protect others.

She watched her go, all alone, up the steps to the empty school, and she wanted more than anything to believe that things were normal. But deep down, she knew they were not. As Scarlet closed the doors behind her, entered that building filled with thousands of kids, Caitlin couldn't help but wonder: were those other kids in there trapped with her? How long would it be until the plague of vampirism spread?

CHAPTER SEVEN

Scarlet ran across the wide stone plaza and up the series of steps to the front doors of her school. As she did, she clutched her light, fall jacket to herself. She wish she'd worn something warmer; just a few days ago, it was like 70, but now, it felt more like 50. October was so unpredictable, she thought. Especially now, at the end, with just a few days before Halloween. She made a mental note in her head that when she got home, she would have to go down to the basement and switch out her late summer wardrobe for her fall one.

Scarlet glanced over her shoulder as she grabbed the front doors, hoping her mom had left. It was so embarrassing, her sitting there like that, watching her, as if she were still in second grade. She cringed as she saw her mom still watching. She hoped that no other kids were watching this, especially given that the school was empty, everyone already in class. She felt so conspicuous.

She didn't really blame her mom for watching her like that, and felt sorry she had scared her—but at the same time she just wanted to put it behind her. Her mom worried too much, and she just wanted her to realize that she was fine, that she was always fine. That even though she was just 16, she was basically a grown woman now, independent, and more than capable of handling herself.

Scarlet burst through the front doors and ran down the hall, her footsteps echoing, her sneakers squeaking on the brightly-polished tile. Her heart raced as she glanced down at her watch and realized second period was almost over. She was so embarrassed: it looked like she'd have to enter class with just a few minutes left; she could already feel the stares. But she didn't have much choice. She couldn't exactly hang out and wait in the hall, especially with the hall monitors patrolling. And she did want to at least make an appearance and maybe grab the homework assignment for the night.

As she hurried down the hall, she wondered once again about what exactly had happened the day before. It really freaked her out, what her parents had told her, that she'd left the house; she couldn't remember that at all. She put on a brave face for everyone, telling them she was fine—and she did feel fine. But inwardly, she was terrified. She was so nervous that she had no memory of it, of where she might've gone. It was terrifying, also, to wake up in the hospital like that. It really shook her. She couldn't stop obsessing over the black hole in her consciousness, over where she went, what she might've done, why they couldn't find her for so long. Had she done anything stupid? Had she seen any of her friends? Had she seen Blake? Why couldn't she remember?

Scarlet felt her cheeks flush as she suddenly recalled what her mom had said: that they'd called the police—and even worse, that they'd called her friends. How mortifying. Who did they call exactly? What did they say? And how would she face everyone? What would all her friends think? And how would she explain it to everyone? She didn't even really understand what had happened herself.

This day would not be easy, she realized, as she neared the classroom door. There'd be a lot of questioning—and she didn't have any answers.

Scarlet finally reached the end of what felt like the longest hall in the school, came to the last door, and grabbed the knob. She braced herself and took a deep breath, clutching her books in one hand, and opened it.

"The algorithm for a triangle that does not exceed—"

Her math teacher stopped writing on the chalkboard, and turned and looked at her. Every other kid in the class looked up at her, too. There were about 30 kids in here, the most boring math class Scarlet had ever had, and luckily, she wasn't friends with most of them.

But there were a few girls in the back that she was friends with, including her best friend, Maria. Scarlet was relieved to see that Maria had kept her seat open for her. Maria was like a sister to her, like the sister she never had; they had known each other since childhood, and were hardly ever apart. Hispanic, with long, brown curly hair and brown eyes, Maria looked a bit, Scarlet always thought, like a young Jennifer Lopez. She was always there for Scarlet when she needed her, and Scarlet was always there for her, too.

But also in the back of the room, Scarlet noticed with dread, were two of the mean, popular girls, including her arch-enemy, Vivian. Scarlet got along with almost everyone—with one exception. Vivian. Five foot nine, with perfectly straight blonde hair, mean blue eyes and a perfect chin and nose, Vivian strutted around the school as if she owned it. A year older than Scarlet, 17, one of the oldest girls in the class, she looked down on everyone. She always wore some kind of variation on a silk blouse, with a small necklace of real, shining pearls. She had pearl earrings to match, and always had perfectly manicured fingernails, in some shade of pink. As beautiful as she was on the outside, she was equally ugly on the inside: she never missed a single opportunity to giggle at someone else, to make fun of them, to take advantage of any moment of weakness.

As Scarlet took another step, right on cue, Vivian let out a loud, mean giggle. That giggle spurred several others to giggle with her, mostly her little group of mean friends. It made a bad situation for Scarlet even worse.

"Sorry I'm late," Scarlet said to the professor, who was still looking at her with wonder.

"You're more than late," he snapped. "The class is almost over. I can't mark you tardy—I'm going to have to mark you absent."

"Fine," Scarlet snapped back at him, then turned and strutted down the aisle, taking the empty seat next to Maria. She hated this math teacher. He was as mean as he was boring. Sometimes she wondered if he and Vivian were distant cousins.

Math was her least favorite subject anyway. She loved to work hard, but if she wasn't interested, she found it really hard to find the motivation. Her favorite class, by far, was English. She loved to read, and lately, she was finding she loved to write, as well. And her English teacher, Mr. Sparrow, was as nice to her as could be. The complete opposite of this math jerk.

The teacher cleared his throat loudly, conspicuously.

"As I was *saying*," he snapped, "when you're dealing with a triangle, the equation between…"

"What happened?" Maria whispered, the second Scarlet took her seat.

Scarlet looked around, waiting for everyone to stop looking at her. Finally, they all turned back to their notes. All, of course, except Vivian: she stared at Scarlet, a condescending smile on her face, as cold as ice. Vivian then leaned over and whispered in her friend's ear, who put her hand to her mouth and giggled. Scarlet could only wonder what she'd said.

"Nothing," Scarlet whispered back to Maria. Scarlet hated hiding anything from her, but she really didn't want talk about it—especially not here, with the teacher waiting to pounce.

Scarlet suddenly felt a vibration in her pocket. She looked down, glanced around to make sure no one was looking, and slid up her cell phone, holding it under her desk. She looked down.

U ok?

It was from Maria.

Scarlet saw Maria furtively holding her phone under her desk with one hand, texting with her thumb, and pretending to take notes while she stared at the blackboard.

Scarlet smiled. She copied Maria, raising one hand and pretending to take notes, while with her thumb, she typed back:

Am fine. Thx.

Scarlet had just hit the send button, when suddenly, the bell rang out.

"Okay class, don't forget, I want chapter three read by tomorrow. And our first quiz is Friday!" the teacher yelled out over the din, as all the kids jumped up, collected their stuff, and headed to the door.

Scarlet got up, collected her things, and walked with Maria out the room.

"OMG, what happened?" Maria asked immediately, barely able to contain herself. "Like, your aunt Polly called me last night. Said they couldn't find you."

Scarlet's heart raced, as she debated how to respond. She didn't want to lie—especially to Maria, who she never held anything back from. But at the same time, she really didn't know what to say, and she needed to diffuse the situation.

"Yeah, they like totally overreacted," she said, thinking quick. "I just went out for a few hours, I forgot my phone, and they couldn't find me."

Scarlet was a bad liar, and wondered if Maria bought it.

"But I heard this morning you were like in the hospital or something," Maria replied skeptically.

Scarlet's heart pounded. That was the downside of living in a small town; she couldn't escape this.

"Yeah...um...well....I got like really sick yesterday after school, and they made me get checked out. But I'm fine."

"Okay, cool," Maria said, and Scarlet felt relieved as it seemed her friend might put it to rest.

They blended out into the loud and crowded hallway, and as they did, Scarlet's sense of dread deepened. She wondered who else would interrogate her, and started to wonder again where she'd actually gone during that time. What if she'd seen one of her friends? What if one of her friends asked her about something she did? Something she couldn't remember? What excuse could she give then?

The halls grew more and more crowded as classes emptied out from every direction. Scarlet and Maria headed down the hall, and as they went, two more of their close friends spotted them and hurried over. They were looking at her in an odd way, and Scarlet braced herself for the questions.

"OMG, what happened to you?" Jasmin asked, hurrying up to her. Black, petite, and filled with energy, Jasmin was one of Scarlet's two other closest friends. At five foot one, with short black hair and large green eyes, Jasmin appeared to be small and frail—but she was actually tough as nails, and prided herself on not being pushed around by anyone and never taking no for an answer. She was fearless, and she always inspired Scarlet, who sometimes wished she could be half as fearless as her. Scarlet loved her, but she could be gossipy, and she never seemed to be able to stop talking. "I heard like, you went missing," she continued. "Like your aunt like called me and I heard the cops were at your place!"

"You OK?" Becca asked.

Scarlet's other friend, Becca, the fourth member of their group, was tall, big-boned, slightly heavyset, with wavy blonde hair. She wasn't quite as attractive as the others, but she had a big heart, was smart as could be, and was a champion soccer player and one of Scarlet's closest friend on the team. She'd also had a steady boyfriend for the last two years, unlike the rest of them. Jasmin was dating someone, too, although only for a few months. Which left Scarlet and Maria—conspicuously—without boyfriends. Maria had just broken up with hers, and Scarlet was hoping Blake would be her boyfriend—though she wasn't sure if he felt the same.

The four of them were nearly inseparable throughout the school day, always finding each other in the hallways—and then usually hanging out at each other's houses after school, too. Maria was her best friend, though, like a true sister, and the two of them were usually

IM-ing or video-chatting when they weren't actually together. Scarlet had other friends, too, but none as close as these three. Their little group wasn't the most popular in the school, but it wasn't the least popular either. They were pretty much average, well-liked, as they were nice to everyone and never made anyone feel left out.

Which was the polar opposite of Vivian's large group of mean girls, that definitely sat at the top of the popularity ranking in the school. Vivian, their ringleader, had at least six friends around her at all times. These girls were always the prettiest, dressed in the most expensive, designer labels, wore the nicest jewelry, carried the nicest bags, always sported the latest line of shoes—and were all cheerleaders. They all seemed to date the hottest guys, the best athletes, and to live in the biggest, nicest houses. They were also always the ones at the center of any school social event, always hosting or organizing the biggest and coolest parties, or anything social the school had to offer.

As if all this weren't enough for them, these girls never seemed happy unless they were also picking on someone else. They had various targets, all throughout the grade, and each of the seven seemed to home in on someone else. Individually, they were annoying—but as a group, they were unbearable, always clustering together and giggling, whispering and pointing, like a pack of hyenas. One never knew exactly what they were talking about, but from their body and facial expressions, it was pretty obvious it wasn't nice.

And God help you if you got in their direct path, if you became a direct rival to any one of them—whether it was in sports, or social situations—or most of all, with boys. Then they would all turn on you like a pack of wolves, and be absolutely determined to make your life in school a living hell.

This was something that Scarlet was just beginning to realize, firsthand, since she had taken an interest in Blake—and especially since they'd gone to the movies the other night. Scarlet had had no idea that Vivian liked Blake, too. Now, she found out the hard way.

In the past, Vivian had always been naturally snotty to Scarlet—but now she stared her down at every turn, and made sure her girlfriends did, too. Now, Scarlet was a direct threat. Of course, it wasn't Scarlet's fault—Blake wasn't dating Vivian, and as far as Scarlet could tell, he wasn't even really that interested in her. But that didn't stop Vivian from blaming Scarlet.

Scarlet braced herself as she spotted Vivian's pack at the far end of the hall. She at least took comfort in her three friends surrounding her, which would shield her from some of their animosity. But despite this, and the distance, she could already spot Vivian whispering and pointing towards Scarlet—and as she did, the group turned as one towards her.

"Hello? So like what happened?" Jasmin pressed. "We're still waiting."

Scarlet realized she hadn't answered their questions.

"Um, sorry…" she said. "It was really no big deal. I just like got sick, and then I went out for a while and lost my phone, and my mom freaked out. Sorry."

"OMG, my mom does that all the time. So embarrassing," Becca chimed in.

Scarlet was visibly relieved to hear her say that. They were buying it.

"But I heard you were like in the hospital or something?" Jasmin pressed.

"Look guys, it was really no big deal," Scarlet said, more firmly. "I'm totally fine. Everyone just over-reacted. Please, can we just talk about something else?" Scarlet pleaded, hearing the stress in her own voice. She didn't mean to snap, but she really wanted them to change the subject. She was also dreading one of them telling her that they spotted her somewhere yesterday, doing something that Scarlet couldn't even remember herself. She hoped and prayed that wasn't the case.

"Well, I'm stressing out," Maria said, "because the dance is in like two days, and I still don't have a date."

Thankfully, as always, she came to Scarlet's rescue and changed the subject. Scarlet was relieved. Yet, at the same time, she had changed the topic to one that was even more stressful: Friday's dance. The big Halloween Ball. Every year, there was a big outdoor dance down on the football field, and the school had a huge bonfire and marshmallow roast. It was the kiss of death to show up without a date. You could get away with it as a freshman, or as a sophomore, but definitely not as a junior or senior. And being a junior, the pressure was really on Scarlet this year.

"Who you bringing?" Jasmin asked. "Blake?" She was clearly trying to pull information out of her. "You never told us what happened on your date!"

Scarlet sighed. This day was going from bad to worse.

"Come on, stop holding back!" Becca said.

Jasmin said Blake's name way too loudly, and had done so at the worst possible moment—right as they were passing the cluster of mean girls. Scarlet looked at Vivian and saw her expression change to a scowl. Clearly, the mention of Blake's name had struck her hard. She could feel the hatred coming off of her.

Scarlet looked away; at least she had safety in numbers.

"Nice shoes," came a snarky voice behind her, followed by a chorus of giggles. It was Vivian's voice, of course.

Scarlet looked down and realized her flats were covered in mud stains. She flushed with embarrassment. Somehow, somewhere, maybe yesterday, she must have ran in the mud. The morning had been such a blur, she hadn't even checked.

"Nice life," Jasmin turned and shot back at Vivian.

Scarlet was so grateful for Jasmin's sticking up for her, and at that moment, she loved her more than ever. But at the same time, she really didn't want to spark a huge confrontation. She just wanted this day to move on.

"At least I have one," Vivian snapped back.

"At least she has a boyfriend," Maria snapped back. "Oh, that's right, I forgot: you don't. Was it supposed to be Blake?"

Scarlet glanced back and saw Vivian's face turn a shade of purple. She was apoplectic. It was obvious that Maria had hit her with the lowest blow of all.

Scarlet was mortified. She hated Vivian, but she definitely didn't want to provoke her like that—especially since she didn't even know if she and Blake were officially dating. She'd made a mistake the other night when she introduced him to her family as her boyfriend—but she had been caught off guard by all of them there, and got nervous, and it just blurted out. She was encouraged he hadn't corrected her—but also nervous that maybe by announcing it like that she might have pushed him away, with too much too soon—especially since they hadn't talked about it. They'd only been on a few dates, and she still wasn't really sure where they stood.

But here her friends were, announcing in front of everyone that Blake was her boyfriend and not Vivian's. It made Scarlet more nervous than ever that this could put Blake on the spot and drive him away; because even though their date was great, she still wasn't really sure how Blake really felt about her. And a part of her was worried that Blake might actually like Vivian—that rubbing it in her face like this might put her into overdrive and force her to do all she could to try to steal Blake away for good.

"Please guys," Scarlet said, grabbing Maria's shoulder and guiding her away, ushering them down the hall.

They turned the corner and reached their lockers, and Scarlet hurried over to hers, quickly opening the lock, throwing her books in and taking out other books she needed. The inside of her locker was covered with cutouts from magazines, a huge collage of pictures that she loved.

Scarlet sighed, trying to gather her thoughts. This day was already ridiculous. It was like a whirlwind. She just wanted to get home, get into bed, curl up with a book, Ruth by her side, and not think about any of this. She felt like she was in a white-hot spotlight, and just wanted to get out of it.

The bell rang, and as Scarlet closed her locker she spotted Blake. Her heart beat faster. He was standing at his locker, about ten rows away. He still hadn't noticed her.

"Go talk to him," whispered Jasmin, gently prodding her back.

That was the prod that Scarlet needed. Without thinking, she took a few steps his way. Her heart was racing.

They'd had such a nice night at the movies. Blake had bought her popcorn and had walked her home, like a gentleman. Scarlet had wondered if he was going to kiss her, and for a moment it seemed like he would. But then it seemed like he'd gotten nervous, and at the last second he kissed her on the cheek instead.

It left Scarlet wondering if he was really into her. Apparently, Scarlet discovered later, he had texted her the following day—but of course, that was the day, of all days, that she had to get sick and go AWOL. She was suddenly flooded with panic as she just realized she'd never replied to his text. Now he must think she'd blown him off.

"Hey," she said, and could hear her own voice trembling.

A few feet away, he turned and looked at her. For a moment, his eyes lit up with joy; but then they clouded over with something like confusion, or hesitation. She couldn't tell what.

"Hey," he said back, sounding surprised. "Are you okay?"

Scarlet felt herself flush.

"Yeah, I'm fine."

"I heard you were like missing or something."

"No, just my mom freaking out," Scarlet said, putting on her best smile. "Parents."

Blake nodded, and slowly smiled. But his expression was inscrutable, and she couldn't tell if he bought it or not. He stood there kind of silent, not igniting any more conversation. She began to worry.

"I texted you yesterday," he said.

Scarlet's heart pounded. He was upset about that.

"Yeah I'm so sorry," she said. "I didn't have my phone all day," she said.

But she feared he might think she was lying. Who didn't have their phone on them all day? She hoped he believed her.

"Well yeah, that's cool," he said, sounding noncommittal.

They stood there in silence, and it was getting awkward. On the one hand, she sensed that he liked her; on the other, he seemed unsure, maybe still hurt about the text. She wanted to make things right, but she didn't know how. Most of all, she wanted to go to the dance with him on Friday—and really wanted him to ask her, and for it to be official that they were boyfriend and girlfriend. Especially before Vivian could try anything.

Scarlet stood there, silently willing for him to say the words: *Will you go to the dance with me on Friday?* She imagined the sound of his voice, his expression as he asked it.

But as they stood, there was just more silence. She felt herself filling with dread.

The bell rang again, and kids began to disperse in every direction. Scarlet's heart sank, as she sensed he was about to head off to class.

But to her surprise, he didn't leave. Instead, he stood there, even as everyone else was swarming around him. He cleared his throat.

"So…um…are you like going to the dance on Friday?" he asked.

Scarlet's heart swelled with relief. It was a huge moment for her, the moment she finally realized he liked her. She heard the shaking in his voice and she realized that he was just nervous. Just like her.

"Well, I—" she began.

"*There* you are," came the voice.

Scarlet wanted to die. There, in front of her, appeared Vivian, slithering up to Blake, wrapping one arm around his.

Blake looked over at her, surprised, ambivalent, clearly unsure how to react.

"I have something really important to talk to you about," Vivian said. "Will you walk me to class?"

Blake stood there, looking back and forth between Vivian and Scarlet, looking trapped, like a deer in the headlights. He looked like he didn't know what to do.

Scarlet could hardly blame him. Vivian stood there, looking so tall, so gorgeous, so perfect, in her perfect makeup and tight-fitting clothes, like a real-life Barbie doll. Beside her, Scarlet felt inadequate. She didn't have her money, or her clothes, or her style, or her perfect, flawless looks. How could she blame Blake for not saying no?

At the same time, Scarlet wanted to scream. Why now, of all times? Why did this creature seem to plague her at every turn? It was almost too much for her to bear. Vivian had everything. Couldn't she just let Scarlet have Blake?

"Um…okay I guess," Blake said to her.

Scarlet examined Blake, looking for any signs of his disliking Vivian. But she couldn't tell; he seemed on the fence, as if he were split right down the middle between Vivian and Scarlet. And that, more than anything, broke Scarlet's heart.

"I guess we'll talk later," he muttered to Scarlet, sounding apologetic as Vivian literally dragged him away.

In moments, the two of them were walking away, down the hall. As they went, Vivian turned and looked back at Scarlet with a mean, victorious smile.

Scarlet stood there and watched them disappear and as she did, she felt her whole world sinking out from under her. She felt as if she had just lost Blake for good.

CHAPTER EIGHT

Scarlet sat in class, fuming. It was so unfair. She wanted to yell at the world. Why couldn't she just have had thirty more seconds with Blake? Why couldn't she have had just enough time for him to respond, for him to ask her to the dance? That was all she needed. Then it would have been too late for Vivian—there was nothing she could have said or done. Now, anything could happen.

God, she hated her. More than anything. She literally stole Blake out from under her, with a second left to go.

And even worse, as luck would have it, Scarlet knew that Blake and Vivian had their next class together. Another stroke of bad luck. If they had just separated after that, if Blake had been in Scarlet's class, then she would have at least had had a chance to set things right. But now Vivian had a full 40 minutes to convince him. Who knew what they were talking about; who knew what she was saying about her. Scarlet felt sure that she wasn't wasting any time, that somehow she would convince Blake to ask her to the dance. *Would he?*

The thought burned Scarlet up inside. She kept replaying in her head all the details of her and Blake's date together. At various points in the movie their elbows and arms had touched, and he hadn't backed away. Neither had she. She felt that he wanted to be closer; but she also felt that he was really nervous. So was she. She wondered once again if she messed up by introducing him to her family as her "boyfriend." Maybe she should have just introduced him as "her friend." But that seemed so awkward and childish, like she was in third grade. Plus, she hadn't wanted them to look at and treat him like any other friend. She had felt a need to draw a line, to be a bit independent, especially from her dad, who could be super protective.

She wished that she hadn't been put in that position to begin with, hadn't been surprised and had to introduce him to everyone. But at the same time, she'd loved having Blake there, and he had seemed like a perfect fit with her family. It had felt so natural.

What would she do if Blake didn't ask her to the dance? And worse: what if he took Vivian? Scarlet would be so embarrassed in front of all her friends, who just moments before were announcing to the world that they were dating.

"Darryl asked Jasmin to the dance," Maria whispered from the seat beside her. "Can you believe it? That leaves only me and you without dates."

Maria must have been reading her mind. Talk of the dance made her stomach drop. The pressure was on, and it was building. Soon, everyone would have a date. Everyone but her.

"So," Maria whispered. "You're leaving me in suspense. Did he ask you?"

Scarlet blinked back at her, for a moment wondering what she was talking about. And then she realized. Blake. She wanted to know if Blake had asked her to the dance.

Scarlet shrugged.

"Um...not really. I mean, he started to, but then Vivian showed up."

"No!" Maria said, eyes opening in disbelief. "What happened?"

"Scarlet and Maria stop speaking right now!" snapped the teacher.

It was another teacher that Scarlet dreaded—her biology teacher. She couldn't think of any subject more boring, and this teacher was a close second in meanness to her math teacher.

But this time, Scarlet welcomed the rebuke. It gave her a chance to regroup, to not have to answer any more questions. She turned and stared out the window, and zoned out all the way until the bell rang.

Scarlet shuffled quickly out the room, Maria by her side, and the two made their way towards the cafeteria, for lunch. As the halls filled with students, surging towards lunch, the energy increased in the air, and the noise got louder. Scarlet started to get nervous as they approached. Blake would be there. He always was. Would he come up to her? Would he ignore her? Would he be sitting with Vivian?

Worse, had Vivian already asked him to the dance? Scarlet didn't think so. As much as Vivian wanted to go with him, it would also be awkward for her to ask. That wouldn't put her in the best light—and it might even backfire.

Scarlet realized this might be her last chance. She had to catch Blake's attention, had to finish their conversation from earlier. Unless, of course, he showed up with Vivian.

"So tell me what happened?" Maria said. "Was he planning to ask you?"

48

"I have no idea," Scarlet snapped back. "Stop asking me."

Scarlet immediately felt bad; she didn't mean to snap at her best friend. All this pressure was just getting to her.

"I'm sorry," she said. "I didn't mean it. I'm just a little stressed, you know?"

Maria nodded gracefully.

"It's okay. I feel it. I'm stressed, too. I think we're the last ones that don't have a date for this thing."

"What about Julio?" Scarlet asked, suddenly remembering Maria's ex-boyfriend. "It looks like you guys are talking again."

"He asked Samantha. Can you believe it? What a pig."

"I'm sorry," Scarlet said, meaning it.

Maria shrugged.

"It's okay. I don't think I would've wanted to go with him anyway. Sometimes you have to let things go, you know what I mean?"

They opened the double doors to the cafeteria, and entered a huge, cavernous room, filled with hundreds of screaming, energetic kids. The tables were packed, and the line for a hot meal wrapped along the wall.

Scarlet spotted Jasmin and Becca sat at a table far across the room, and as she walked over to them, she scanned the room for any signs of Blake or Vivian. There were none. She did, though, notice that Blake was absent from his usual table of friends—and so was Vivian. Not a good sign. Were the two of them together somewhere?

Scarlet sat at her table, her heart thumping, and set down her books.

"Hey guys."

"Hey."

"The meatloaf's good today," Becca said.

But Scarlet wasn't hungry. Her heart was fluttering, and she was finding it hard to concentrate. Maria dragged her to the line with her, and she found herself waiting on it with all the others.

"Maybe I just won't go," Maria said, as they reached the food and the women heaped huge servings of food on their trays. "I mean, what's the big deal about a dance anyway? It's so overblown. It's just a huge pressure cooker. And it's always so lame. There's that bonfire, and most people don't even dance."

"I know," Scarlet agreed.

"I mean, who made up this stupid dance anyway?" Maria continued, as they took their trays and headed back to the table. "It's like just a big excuse for everyone to see who's dating who. It's so aggravating."

As they headed back, Scarlet saw something that made her heart leap: there, sitting at the table with all the popular girls, was Vivian. As Scarlet walked past, Vivian looked up and glared at her, daggers in her eyes. There was no sign of Blake, anywhere.

That was a good sign. The two of them were not together, and Vivian was pissed. Maybe something went wrong. Clearly, Vivian hadn't been successful yet; if she had, she'd be sporting a smile. At least now Scarlet had a chance.

Scarlet smiled inwardly to herself as she made her way back to her table with her food, sitting with the others.

She sat there, food untouched, watching the door, as more and more kids streamed in, looking for any sign of Blake. She saw his table, with all his friends, and he still wasn't there. He had to come in any second. And when he did, she would make room for him, try to get him to sit with her. In fact, she prepared, sliding over.

"What are you doing?" Maria asked, looking at the empty seat as Scarlet slid over.

Scarlet had no time to explain: suddenly, she saw him, walking through the door. Blake looked as cute as ever. He walked in with a big smile on his face, carrying a small bag of lunch, skipping the line. He was walking in her direction, right at her, and as she looked up, their eyes locked. He saw her. She was sure of it.

Scarlet began to get up as Blake walked right for her table. He was only a few feet away and he wasn't even looking at his guy friends. He was looking at her. Clearly, he was coming to sit with her.

"Blake?" came the voice.

No, Scarlet though. *Not again.*

Blake stopped, a few feet away, and turned at the harsh voice summoning him.

Vivian stood at the head of the table of girls, gesturing to him at an empty seat beside the head of their table.

"I saved you a seat," she said.

It was more like a command than a request—and her entire group of friends, in perfect solidarity, all stared at him as one, in such a way that left open no room for refusal. It was a look that said: if you

50

don't sit here with us now, you are forever banned from the popular group.

Blake stopped. He turned and looked helplessly at Scarlet, and she could see the hesitation in his eyes, see that he didn't have the willpower to say no. His shining eyes darkened, as he turned reluctantly and made his way, as if in a trance, over to Vivian's table.

As he sat, Vivian turned and glared at Scarlet, gave her the meanest smile she could, then sat down with Blake.

"That witch," Maria said, as she watched what happened. "I hate her."

"Someone should poison her soup," Jasmin added.

Slowly, Scarlet sat back down, feeling humiliated. Becca reached over and put arm on her shoulder.

"It's okay girl," she said. "If he wants her, let him have her. You're too good for him. And for her. He'll get exactly what he deserves."

Scarlet sat there, staring down at her mound of meatloaf, gravy cold, and felt completely numb. She felt her face redden as she felt as if the entire room had witnessed the scene. Vivian had stolen Blake right out from under her, in the most public way, for the second time this morning. She couldn't help but feel as if her fate with him had been sealed. It was obvious she wasn't going to the dance at this point.

Scarlet couldn't help thinking back to the other night, to Blake's being at her house, to what a good time they'd had together—and she felt even worse. Maybe she didn't deserve Blake. After all, who was she? She guessed that some people considered her attractive, but in her own mind, at least, she didn't consider herself to have the looks of a girl like Vivian.

"It's okay," Scarlet muttered under her breath.

"It's *not* okay," Jasmin said, angry. "We're going to find a way to get her back. Just wait and see. She better watch her back."

"Don't worry," Becca said. "There are plenty of fish in the sea. I'm sure there are a ton of guys who'd love to go with you."

"Guys, it's fine, really," Scarlet said. "I'm not a charity case."

"What about Dave?" Jasmin asked.

Scarlet shook her head. Dave was a nice guy, but she wasn't attracted to him at all, despite his trying to follow her around whenever he could.

"Dances are overrated anyway," Scarlet said, softly.

"Exactly my point," Maria said.

"You'll feel differently once you meet the right guy," Becca said.

"OMG, did you guys hear? About the new kid?" Jasmin suddenly said, switching the topic.

They all turned and stared at her. Jasmin had a way of always being on the cutting edge of the latest gossip, and a way of delivering a story that always put people on the edge of their seats. She also had an annoying way of drawing out suspense as long she possibly could, savoring the attention.

"I heard it from Leslie, who heard it from Cindy. Today's his first day. OMG, he's supposed to be GORGEOUS. As in drop-dead. He transferred here. Nobody knows from where. He's from, like, a super-rich family. They've got this huge mansion on the river."

"I heard something about him," Becca said. "Darlene was talking about him this morning. She said he's a senior. Tall, really hot."

"I heard he already has a girlfriend," chimed in Maria.

"That's not true. Cindy told me he's definitely single," Jasmin said.

"Won't be long until he's snatched up," Becca added.

"My God, do you think he's going to the dance? You think he already has a date?"

"You kidding? He just got here. How could he? But he will. I hear Vivian's crowd is already trying to snatch him up. They've like already invited him to parties and one of them already asked him—"

Suddenly, the murmuring in the cafeteria grew quiet. Everybody in the room turned, looked towards the door.

There, walking alone through the double doors, was the most beautiful boy Scarlet had ever seen. About six feet tall, with broad shoulders and long-ish brown hair, he had a proud jaw, a straight nose, and large, gray eyes. He had such a proud, noble face, like an ancient Roman warrior. As he strutted into the room, Scarlet felt like he was royalty or something.

He looked too glamorous to be in this room, like he belonged on the cover of a magazine. And he walked with such confidence, he looked like the only man in a room full of boys—though his face looked young, ageless. In fact, there was something to his face, something mysterious, other-worldly. His skin was so polished, so perfect, it looked radiant.

"O—M—G," Maria whispered to the others, as the chatter in the room slowly picked up again, as the boy strutted across the room, to the food line. "That is BY FAR the hottest guy I've ever seen. OMG," she said again.

As Maria turned back to the table, Scarlet could see she was so flustered, her face had turned bright red. She was sweating. She reached up and wiped her forehead with her hand, then waved herself as if trying to get air. "I think I'm dreaming."

"You're not," Becca said. "I saw it, too."

"He's mine," Maria said. "There is my date."

"Are you kidding?" Jasmin said. "Every girl in the school's gonna want him."

"What are you saying, I can't compete?" Maria shot back.

"No—I'm just saying—I mean, like, good luck. You might be up against everyone."

"I'll find a way," Maria said.

"How do you know he doesn't already have a girlfriend?" Becca asked. "I mean, he looks older than everyone. Maybe he's like dating someone outside of school. Maybe like someone in college or something."

"I don't care," Maria said. "Am I dreaming, or have you never seen a guy that hot in your life?"

They all nodded in agreement, looking over and watching him at the food line. Scarlet could see in their faces they all wished they were dating him, too.

As Scarlet sat there, watching him at the food line, she couldn't help but feel the same way. There was something about this boy: every move he made, every gesture, was so graceful, so noble. So proud. The way he moved, it was so smooth, so different from everyone around him. And when he smiled back at the serving people, she saw rows of gleaming white teeth, his perfect jaw line, and the most beautiful smile she'd ever seen. For a moment, all thoughts of Blake left her mind.

As he reached the register and paid, he picked up his tray and surveyed the room. Scarlet could see hundreds of eyes staring back at him, then quickly looking away, pretending not to look.

For a second, Scarlet saw him look their way, at her table. And then, for the briefest moment, she thought they locked eyes.

She couldn't believe it. Her heart started pounding in her chest. Was this really happening?

"Oh my God," Maria said, "he's looking at me. Do you see him? He's looking at me!"

Maria was sitting close to Scarlet, and Scarlet felt certain he was staring at her, not at Maria. But she didn't have the heart to say anything. And besides, Maria had made it clear how much she wanted this boy, and Maria was her best friend.

So, as smitten as she was, Scarlet forced herself to look away, to look anywhere but at him. She prided herself on being a loyal friend, no matter what.

The boy slowly crossed the room, walking past their table.

"OMG, he's heading this way," Maria said, flustered. Scarlet had never seen her that flustered before. She was acting as if she were in the presence of a celebrity.

He walked past their table, and Scarlet made a point to look away, to make sure that their eyes did not meet again. After he passed, she waited several seconds, then glanced over, and looked to see where he went. He sat at an empty table, at the far end of the cafeteria, by himself, his back to all the others.

"Okay, now's your chance," Jasmin said to Maria. "He's sitting there, all alone. Make your move."

But Maria was totally flustered.

"You crazy?" she said. "Everyone's watching. I can't just like walk over there by myself and try to pick him up."

"Why not?" Jasmin said. "You just said you wanted to."

Maria slumped.

"What if he like…says no?" she asked. Scarlet could hear how scared she sounded.

"Chicken," Jasmin goaded.

"I'm not chicken," she said.

But at the same time, Maria just sat there, frozen, a shade of crimson, too terrified to cross the room and go to him.

Scarlet couldn't blame her. The entire school would be watching her, and if she got rejected, she would never live it down.

Scarlet couldn't bear to turn and look at the boy, either. But for a very different reason.

Because, for the first time in her life, Scarlet knew she had just seen the boy that she was destined to be with forever.

CHAPTER NINE

Caitlin sat at her breakfast table in the large house, late in the morning, all alone, trying to will her life to return to normal. It was not easy. She was still shaking inside, and had been ever since she'd dropped Scarlet off at school. She just couldn't bring herself to work today, and had called in sick. Ruth alone had kept her company, Caleb long gone at work. Not that his presence here would have given her much solace: since their big argument in the hospital, they were hardly on speaking terms.

Caitlin didn't know what to make of all of this. She and Caleb never argued before. This was all new to her, and it couldn't have come at a worse time. Now, more than ever, was when she needed him here, by her side, to tell her that everything was all right. That she was not crazy. That he had seen it, too. That he understood what she was going through. That he agreed that Scarlet needed to be seen by experts. That something had to be done. That they couldn't just sit there and wait for the worst, deny that something awful was unfolding before their eyes.

But it was obvious that Caleb was not on her side. He was taking the side of the rational, the conventional, insisting that everything was normal, that nothing unusual had ever happened. Like that stupid doctor in the hospital, with all his stupid rationale. *Conversion Syndrome.* It was ridiculous.

Of course, there was a part of Caitlin that wanted desperately to believe it, to cling onto something. But that would be too easy. She had been in that room. She had seen with her own eyes what Scarlet had done. She had heard her snarl, had seen Caleb go flying across the room. That was not Conversion Syndrome. That was not an adrenaline rush. It was supernatural.

Caitlin refused to let the establishment brainwash her, convince her that she hadn't seen what she saw. Something was happening to her daughter. And she felt she desperately needed help. She wouldn't go to work, wouldn't pretend all was normal—wouldn't even allow herself to think of anything else—until all this was resolved. The thought of it consumed her.

Not to mention, of course, her journal. How could she ignore that, too? After she'd returned from the hospital, the first thing she did was re-read it. She had to know that this was real, that she wasn't crazy. The more she read it, the more she felt certain. Here she was, holding something real. Holding something that even a scholar like Aiden couldn't explain away. And of course, it was Aiden, a scholar, an authority figure, who had insisted that this was all true. That Scarlet would turn into a vampire.

If Caitlin hadn't found the journal, if she hadn't met with Aiden, if Aiden hadn't told her what he had, then maybe now she could be more easily convinced, could dismiss it all as Caleb had. But knowing this, there was no way she could let it go. A part of her wondered whether she should show her journal to Caleb, tell him about her meeting with Aiden—but she knew that would just further isolate him, just make him certain she was crazy. Whether he believed her or not didn't matter to her anymore. She was strong enough to do this alone—and she would do whatever she had to to rescue her daughter.

A part of her was burning to call Aiden, to get him on the phone, to meet with him, to hear him out. Now she wanted to know more, to know everything and anything he could tell her. She desperately wanted his mentoring, his advice. And she desperately wanted to talk to someone who would make her feel that she wasn't crazy.

But she thought again of his final words, that she must stop her daughter, and recalled his expression. She felt he was suggesting that she kill Scarlet, sacrifice her daughter for the greater good of humanity. And that was something that she could not—that she could never—entertain. She was afraid that if she called Aiden now, he would only suggest the same thing, and the thought of it made her so sick, she couldn't bear to talk to him.

So instead, she put down her cell phone, and tried to think of another way. She felt a call to action, but the problem was, she didn't know what. What could she possibly do? Bring her to more doctors? What would they say? Suggest Scarlet see a psychiatrist? Or would they send her to an adrenaline expert? A sleep expert?

Of course, all that was ridiculous. It would be useless. That was not what Scarlet needed. What she really needed, Caitlin knew, was an expert in the paranormal. Someone who knew what she was going through, someone who knew a way to heal her. To rid her of this. To make her go back to being a normal teenage girl.

But Caitlin didn't know anyone like this. She had absolutely no idea where to turn.

She reached down and stroked Ruth's head; Ruth closed her eyes appreciatively, and rested her chin on her lap. Caitlin looked around their beautiful dining room, and everything seemed so perfect, so normal. Nothing seemed out of place. The sun streamed in through the windows, and it was hard to believe that anything could be wrong in the world. For a moment, Caitlin desperately wanted to pretend that none of this ever happened.

She reached out and picked up the full glass of juice before her, her hand trembling. She took a deep breath, put it to her dry and cracked lips, and drank. It felt good. She realized it was almost lunchtime and this was the first food or drink she'd had all day. She put down the juice and reached over and sipped her coffee, now cold. But it still felt good, and she drank nearly the entire thing. She went to work on her cold eggs, and as she ate she slowly felt her energy return. Ruth whined, and Caitlin took one of her pieces of turkey bacon, leaned over, and fed it to her. She chewed it happily, the noise of the crunching bacon filling the air, making Caitlin smile.

For a moment, Caitlin wondered if maybe things could go back to normal. Maybe, if she did nothing, things might just settle down by themselves. Maybe, like Caleb said, she was just working herself up. And after all, what could she possibly do anyway? She took another deep breath, and started to wonder if maybe the best course of action was to do nothing and deal with things as they happened. Maybe if there was another incident, Caleb would believe her, and would help bring Scarlet to doctors or whoever else she needed. The thought filled her with a strange sense of relief.

Starting to feel better, Caitlin reached over and raised the local morning paper, folded crisply on the table. She leaned back in her chair and opened it, as she always did, and for just a brief second, she almost fell life returning to normal. She was starting to feel good for the first time that morning, when suddenly she read the headline on the front page.

Her stomach plummeted. She sat straight up, and all thoughts of normalcy fled from her mind.

LOCAL GIRL ATTACKED BY ANIMAL

Around midnight last night, a local girl, Tina Behler, 16, a junior at Rhinebeck High, was found unconscious by police on Main Street. She was reported to have been found in a fit of hysteria, wailing that an animal had attacked her. The police could find no visible signs of attack, but brought her to a local hospital for treatment.

Authorities are still puzzled as to whether it was an animal attack or not, and what sort of animal. Residents are urged to be cautious in exiting their homes at night, until authorities resolve this matter.

"We feel confident that if an animal attacked her, it was an isolated incident, and not one that could be of harm to other residents," officer Hardy said. "There are no reports of any animals loose from local zoos, or of any local wildlife."

Caitlin stood, palms sweating, as she read the rest of the article. Finally, she set the paper down, hands shaking worse than they had been before.

An animal attack. Late last night. Just three blocks from her house. At the same time that Scarlet had been out there, unaccounted for.

Could Scarlet have done this? Caitlin wondered.

Her heart was pounding in her throat. It was too much of a coincidence. She wanted to believe more than anything that Scarlet had nothing to do with it—but deep down, she felt she had. Scarlet had probably attacked someone. Turned someone. The officers probably hadn't seen the small bite marks in the throat. Or maybe they were keeping it quiet. And this poor girl was probably going to change. Become like Scarlet. Attack more people. And spread this throughout the town. They would spread it throughout the county. Then the state. Then the country—and then the world.

Caitlin was wracked with guilt. Had she unwittingly allowed it all to happen?

Without even stopping to think, she picked up her cell phone, took officer Hardy's card from the night before, and dialed him. He had said to call him anytime. This was her chance to take him up on it.

"Officer Hardy?" Caitlin asked.

"Yes?"

"This is Caitlin Paine. Scarlet's mother?"

"Oh yes, Mrs. Paine, how are you? I'm glad to hear that Scarlet turned up okay. She is okay, isn't she?" he added, suddenly wary.

Caitlin paused, wondering how to respond.

"Yes, the doctors say she is healthy and normal, and she's back in school."

"Well that's good news. I can use good news right now. Last night was a crazy night. You saw the papers, I take it?"

"Actually, that's why I'm calling. I'm so concerned for that poor girl. I'm wondering if you could tell me more. What happened?"

He paused.

"Why do you want to know?" he asked warily. "Do you think Scarlet is somehow connected to this event?"

"Oh no, nothing like that," Caitlin said quickly, trying to cover her tracks. "I just…well, I knew the girl," she said, lying. "She was a family friend. And I guess I'm just wondering if she's OK. And of course, wondering what attacked her—and if it's safe to go outside."

"Well, I'm really not at liberty to discuss all the details," he said. He paused, though, and then lowered his voice, "but if you can keep it just between us, I'll tell you, there is no animal. Nothing to worry about."

Caitlin paused, surprised.

"What do you mean?"

He paused, then finally continued.

"She was hysterical. Screaming her head off—and screaming the craziest things. But the doctors gave her a full workup, and she was fine. No signs of any animal attack whatsoever. Not even a scratch. In fact, just between us, this morning they transferred her to a psych ward. She was really out-of-control. That's where she is now. No visitors anyway, so you couldn't see her even if you wanted to. Kids these days. It's really sad. I'll bet it was a bad drug trip."

Caitlin's heart pounded at the thought of this poor girl, locked away.

"How long will she be there?" she asked. She was secretly wondering when she might be released, and if she was turned, when she might inflict damage on others.

"I have no idea," he said. "Things like this don't happen around here. Like I said, a crazy night. Must have been a full moon. I'm sorry Ms. Paine, have another call coming in. Is there anything else?"

"No, thanks very much."

The phone went dead.

Caitlin's hands were trembling as she hung up the phone. It had confirmed her worst fears. A girl, attacked, late at night, just a few blocks away, where her daughter was.

She ran across the room, grabbing her journal, turning back its pages once again. She had to remind herself that this was all real, that she wasn't losing her mind. She read from it again:

And then everything happened. So fast. My body. Turning. Changing. I still don't know what happened, or who I've become. But I know I'm not the same person anymore.

I remember that fateful night when it all began. Carnegie Hall. My date with Jonah. And then...intermission. My....feeding? Killing someone? I still can't remember. I only know what they told me. I know that I did something that night, but it's all a blur. Whatever I did, it still sits like a pit in my stomach. I'd never want to harm anyone.

The next day, I felt the change in myself. I was definitely becoming stronger, faster, more sensitive to light. I smelled things, too. Animals were acting strangely around me, and I felt myself acting strangely around them.

This was her own handwriting. There was no doubt. This was real. She had to believe that it was all real. That her daughter was like her. A vampire.

Caitlin couldn't just sit there. She had to do something. The inaction was driving her crazy, and she felt herself bouncing off the walls. She racked her brain, desperately trying to think of what to do, who to talk to next.

And then, suddenly, as she saw the cross mounted on the wall above the table, it hit her: a priest. If anyone was qualified to know anything about the paranormal, about vampires, about the spiritual forces of good and evil, it would be a priest. The local priest, Father McMullen, was a good, kind man. She didn't know him that well, but she knew enough to know he was accepting. He was the perfect person to talk to; he could not only give her comfort, but also give her guidance, tell her if she was crazy, and if not, tell her what to do. After all, the church still had an exorcism ritual, didn't they? Maybe they had a ritual for vampires? Or at least, maybe they knew of one?

Without wasting another second she crossed the room, grabbed her coat and keys and hurried through the house, taking the steps three at a time as she ran outside.

*

Caitlin walked down the bluestone walkway, crossing a huge expanse of lawn to the gothic church. Built two centuries ago, its steeple rising a hundred feet, the church towered over everything in this small town. Its exterior was ornate, gargoyles protruding from every side, elaborate stonework framing a grand, arched door; it looked like it belonged in a capital city of Europe, in another era. It was one of Caitlin's favorite things about this town—and she especially loved that she lived just a few blocks away.

Oddly, she hardly ever came here—only a handful of times since she had lived here—yet she still felt comforted by its presence as she walked past it every day, and by the sound of its bells. She would often open her bedroom window at night, and fall asleep to the sound of its chimes, which rang out to the abridged tunes of various classical composers.

She also really liked the priest. She had only met him a handful of times over the years, but each time had left a great impression. He was young, in his 40s, tall and slim, with a kind, compassionate face and longish, sandy brown hair, freckles on his cheeks matching the color of his hair. He was soft-spoken, quick to smile, and self-effacing. He always shook everybody's hands with two of his, clasping their hands warmly, embracing them in his own. The few times she had sought him out, like when she was upset she was unable to have a second child, he had always managed to make her feel better. Caitlin felt that she could tell him anything.

The large oak door creaked as she opened it, and her eyes adjusted from the bright sunlight of the day to the dim interior. As she stepped in, she realized the church was completely empty—of course, it would be, at lunchtime on a weekday—and she suddenly felt self-conscious. She felt as if she were walking into someone's home unannounced, as if the door were only unlocked by accident. It was a grand interior, the arched ceilings rising a hundred feet, filled with stained-glass and with endless wooden pews, all empty. The floors were comprised of large slabs of dark stone, well-worn, with a wide aisle which led to an elaborate altar, backed by stained-glass windows.

"Hello?" Caitlin called out tentatively, her voice echoing.

She waited. There was no response.

"Father McMullen?" she called out, louder.

Her voice echoed back to her, with no response.

Slowly, her eyes began to adjust to the dim interior. A passing cloud lifted, revealing the sun, which flooded the stained glass in different colors. The muted light was peaceful in here: it felt timeless, like a sanctuary. As if all her troubles were left behind those doors.

Caitlin wondered if she should leave. But it was hard to walk away. A part of her felt comforted being here; for some reason, she felt some sort of connection to being in a church, even though she wasn't particularly religious. She couldn't understand it. She could count on her fingers the number of times she had been in one. Yet every time she entered one, she felt some sort of mysterious connection to her past. She thought of her vampire journal. Were those real memories?

She found herself walking slowly down the aisle, her footsteps echoing, gravitating towards the altar. At the end was an enormous cross, covered in gold foil, and as she walked closer, she was suddenly struck with memories, flashbacks. She saw herself walking down an aisle, in a grand church, Caleb by her side. She saw herself in one church after the next, each more and more elaborate, in England, Scotland, Italy, France. She saw herself in the Notre Dame in Paris. In the Duomo in Florence. In Westminster Abbey. In each, Caleb was by her side. She suddenly saw her and Caleb's wedding. She saw them standing before a castle, in Scotland, hundreds of people in attendance, walking down an aisle covered in rose petals. She saw a sky lit up by the most beautiful sunset she had ever seen. It was magical.

She opened her eyes and wondered if that had all been a fantasy? She stood before the altar, staring at the shining, gold cross, and tried to focus. She felt connected to this cross. To Jesus. She couldn't understand why. The thought of Jesus being her father in heaven was reassuring to her somehow. Was that because she had never known her father in real life?

She forced herself to focus on Scarlet. She felt waves of desperation overcome her, and found herself clasping her hands in prayer. She was desperate for help, and she silently prayed for a miracle.

She felt weak. She went to the pews and sat a few rows from the front. As she did, she looked up and noticed an open Bible. It was a thick book, and the header read: *The New Testament, The Book of Luke*. She scanned the pages, looking for a sign, wondering if her prayer had been answered. She read:

"I grant you power and authority over every demon, power and authority over every disease."

Her heart raced. Was it a message?

She propped her elbows on the bench before her, rested her face in her hands, and silently prayed. She prayed for help for Scarlet. For herself. For her family. She had never felt so alone, so desperate. She was soon crying. She felt like a broken woman. All the tension, all the stress of the last few days—her almost losing Scarlet, her fighting with Caleb, her meeting with Aiden—all came pouring out. Her cries filled the air.

"My child," came a soft voice.

Caitlin turned and saw Father McMullen, approaching her from the far side of the room. He crossed the cavernous room, his footsteps echoing, and Caitlin stood, embarrassed. She smoothed her skirt, and wiped the tears from her cheeks.

"I'm sorry father, I didn't mean to barge in like this," she said, her voice shaking. "I realize you're probably not open now—"

He raised a palm to stop her, as he broke into a soft, warm smile.

"We are always open," he said. "It's Caitlin, isn't it? Caitlin Paine?"

She nodded back, impressed he remembered.

"I never forget a face," he said. "I am more than happy to see you here. I am sorry I was not here to greet you personally. You caught me on my lunch break," he added with a smile.

Caitlin smiled, reassured at his presence. He held out his palm, and she shook his hand. She felt warmth and reassurance as he clasped her hand in both of his and smiled warmly.

"I'm sorry," she said, wiping away her tears.

He shook his head. "There is nothing to be sorry for. Our Lord in heaven appreciates heartfelt prayer."

Caitlin sensed that she had come to the right place, that he was exactly the one she should talk to. She sighed, feeling some tension leaving her body.

"Would you like to talk?" he asked softly, after a few moments of silence.

"Yes, I would," she replied.

"Let's take a walk," he said, and turned and led her across the room. "It's a bit impersonal in here. Have you seen our new courtyard? It's a gorgeous day, and everything is in bloom, and with the leaves falling, it's a medley of color. I think you'll find it heartwarming."

"I'd like to see that," she said, as they continued across the huge room.

He didn't say anymore, didn't press her with questions, and she sensed he was waiting for her to open up. She appreciated, more than he would ever know, his giving her time and space to collect herself. Clearly, this was a man who didn't pry.

"I'm sorry I haven't come here more often," she said. "I live practically down the block. I hope you're not offended."

He smiled.

"I'm happy that you're here now. The present is all we have, isn't it? All of our mistakes, all of our regrets—all that we've done in the past—it's nothing compared to the power of the present. Thank you for coming now."

He stepped to the side and opened the door for her. They continued down a stone corridor, leading towards the rear courtyard.

"I'm afraid I'm not very good with confession," Caitlin said. "I don't even know what it is, really. I don't think I've ever done it—or at least properly. I'm not really sure what to say—"

"Don't worry about any of that," he said reassuringly. "Just speak from your heart. Tell me whatever you want to tell me."

They walked out into a small courtyard in the back of the church. It was beautiful, quaint, filled with blooming fall flowers of every variety and a small pumpkin patch, and framed by large, reassuring, ancient trees, their leaves a medley of color, many of which were sprinkled in the garden. They followed a narrow, stone pathway and made their way to a bench beneath a tree.

They sat side by side and Caitlin leaned back, feeling at ease for the first time in days. A cool October breeze caressed her, taking off the heat of the sun. All around her, birds were chirping.

They sat there in silence for what felt like forever. Not once did the Father intrude on her thoughts. Clearly, this was a patient man, well-trained in the art of listening.

Caitlin didn't quite know how to begin.

"My daughter, Scarlet, is sick," she finally said.

He turned to her, looking back with caring eyes.

"What's wrong with her?"

"Yesterday—" she began, then stopped. *My God, was it only yesterday?* she thought. It felt like years had passed. "Yesterday…she came home sick from school. Then…she ran out of the house. She was missing, until today. We found her in the morning, and took her to the hospital. She was fine. The doctors say she's fine. But I don't feel that she's fine."

"What's wrong with her?" he asked again.

Caitlin sighed, trying to figure how to phrase it. She wanted to stop beating around the bush.

"Father, do you believe in the paranormal?" she asked.

He turned and really looked at her for the first time, and she could see his green eyes widen in surprise. He looked away.

"If by that you mean, do I believe there are spiritual and unexplained forces beyond the physical realm? Yes, I do. I do not believe that we live in just a physical realm. There are clearly things in God's universe that are meant to be unexplained. Things which we were never meant to understand."

"But do you believe in the…supernatural?" Caitlin asked. "I mean—for example—the Catholic Church—it believes in spirits, right? Demons? Possession? Exorcism? I mean—you have exorcism rituals, don't you?"

He shifted in his seat and rubbed his palms on his knees, and she could sense he was uncomfortable. He cleared his throat.

"Officially, yes. There is a ritual in the Catholic Church for exorcism. Have I ever seen it in practice? No. Have I ever practiced it myself? No. It is a very rare thing. As much as it may have been dramatized in the movies," he said with a smile, "it is something you really never hear about." He paused. "Why do you ask?"

Caitlin collected her thoughts. She wanted to say the right thing, and didn't want to seem crazy.

"I guess what I'm asking you is…do *you* believe in it? Do you believe that such a thing can exist?"

He blinked, and she could see him thinking. He was silent for a long time.

Finally, he took a deep breath.

"Yes. Personally, I do. Over my years, I have certainly encountered things which I could not explain. What I like to think of as intense, spiritual moments. Moments where people's spirits defied their bodies, and vice versa. There is a spiritual realm. And yes, of course, where there is light, there is darkness—and there can be a dark side to the spiritual realm, as well. In my view, though, light is stronger than darkness—and all darkness can be conquered by the light."

He paused, looking at her.

"Why do you ask? Are you concerned for your daughter? Has something happened to her?"

Caitlin decided she had to tell him. She had no choice, and she felt she could trust him.

"I don't believe that my daughter is possessed, no," she said. "I know this whole conversation must sound crazy, forgive me—"

He held up a palm.

"Please. I don't judge. You would not believe the things I see and hear. Nothing surprises me, and I'm open to anything."

Caitlin sighed, feeling better.

"I don't believe that Scarlet is possessed, no. But I do think she is suffering from something that is not…physical, for lack of a better word. You see, father," she said, and dropped her voice, "I believe that my daughter is becoming a vampire."

He stared back at her, his eyes opening twice as wide. He looked startled. But, to Caitlin's relief, she didn't sense he was dismissing her.

He sat there for several moments, as he looked out at the garden in amazed silence.

"I'm not crazy, father. I'm a scholar. I have a beautiful, loving family. I've been a member of this community for years. I…I…"

Caitlin suddenly lowered her head into her hands and started to cry, realizing how crazy she sounded.

To her surprise, she felt a reassuring hand on her back.

"There is no need to explain, or apologize. I don't judge you."

She looked up at him, through teary eyes.

"But do you believe me? Do you believe it's possible? That vampires can exist?"

He sighed and looked away.

"It's complicated," he said. "There is a long and complex history between the paranormal and the Catholic Church. Over the centuries, some factions have discounted it as absurd; others have acknowledged it. The official position now is somewhere in between. Exorcism is safer ground. But when you deal with other…forms of the supernatural…it is a very fine line."

"But what do *you* believe?" Caitlin pressed.

He stared silently out at the courtyard.

"It's odd you should ask me this question, because my own doctorate was on the history of the paranormal and the church. I happen to know the history of it, from a scholarly perspective, very well. If you look at the literature, the records, what's remarkable about the vampire legend is that it persists—not just for a century or two, but for thousands of years. That would be remarkable in and of itself, but even more remarkable is that the vampire legend has existed in nearly every culture in the world, in every geographical location, every language. Even in ancient times, you find recorded entries of vampire myths and legends, even some supposed documented occurrences, in languages ranging from Chinese to African, and in places that were never geographically connected. That, of course, makes it not so easy to explain away."

He paused, taking a deep breath.

"Even harder to explain away is that there appear common threads to the legends. Nearly always, it has to do with the body of someone recently interred. With a body rising again. Almost always, the soul has died in a way which was unharmonious—a suicide, or murder, for example. Someone who had left the earth in a way of great calamity. In the legends, these unsettled souls rise again, after burial. In some legends, they merely visit their families; in others, they are more aggressive, and seek out blood. Blood is the common theme."

He sighed again.

"Of course, viewed from another light, blood is a recurring theme in Catholicism, too. The blood of Christ. The sipping of the wine. The holy Grail. The drink that promises immortality. In this light, one could argue that these legends and fables are intertwined with Catholic doctrine in a disturbing way."

"What are you saying?" Caitlin asked, excited. "As you saying that you believe they exist? Now, in the modern day and age?"

He sighed.

"Again, it's not so simple. Historically, there were many forms of vampires. Not just a physical one—but emotional and even psychic vampires. I do believe in emotional and psychic vampirism. We see it every day, all around us. A person who, for example, vents on a co-worker with all of their troubles, and the co-worker leaves feeling deflated. That is emotional vampirism. One has fed on the other."

"But what about the other kind?" she asked. "Physical vampires?"

He slowly shook his head.

"It is not that I discount it, necessarily. It is that I have yet to see an example of it with my own eyes. I've seen horrible, awful things. I've seen perfectly healthy people have psychotic breaks. Completely unexplained. Could this be accounted to demonic possession? Yes. Could it be accounted to vampirism? Perhaps. In my view, it doesn't really matter what you label it. What you have is an unexplained event that is outside the guise of normal—thus, *para*-normal.

"Do I believe there exist in the universe dark spiritual forces that can sway a normal human life? Yes. If you would like to call that vampirism, you could. But I would view it more along the lines of possession. In other words—I would view it as a dark spiritual force that could be exorcised. I believe that God is all-powerful, and that any force on this earth which is not positive, can be healed through God's light."

Caitlin's eyes opened wide, as she felt herself fill with hope for the first time.

"Can you heal my daughter?"

He looked back at her, long and hard.

"First, remember that I am not a healer."

"But you have healed people. I mean, you have helped them, at least. You help them every day."

"Yes, I have helped people. Whether I can help her…I would have to meet her before I could say," he said. "But I don't feel that anything is impossible. I don't know if I can heal her," he said, "but I do have faith that she can be healed. Whatever her ailment."

Caitlin stared back at him, welling with hope.

"Please, father. I would give anything. Please, please help my daughter."

He stared back at her, long and hard. Finally, he said:

"Bring her to me."

CHAPTER TEN

Sage pulled the huge, iron gate closed behind him, rattling as it slammed shut, then began his walk down the endless driveway towards his family mansion, upset with himself. They had asked him to fulfill a simple mission, for the sake of his entire clan. And he had sincerely intended to. But once he had seen her—Scarlet—everything had changed. He could not possibly bring himself to do what they asked.

He walked slowly, kicking the dirt, eyes on his toes, thinking. The driveway stretched as far as the eye could see, lined with huge, old oak trees, branches arching over it, almost touching, their leaves creating a medley of color. Sage felt as if he were walking into a postcard on this beautiful, late-October day, leaves crunching beneath his feet, the late afternoon sun bouncing off of everything. On the one hand, it made him happy to be alive.

But on the other, it sent a pain to his stomach, as it made him more aware of his own mortality than ever. After all these centuries, he was now faced with only a few weeks left to live. He knew he must savor each day more than ever, savor every site, every smell, taste, experience—knowing it would all be his last. He wanted to hold onto everything, but he felt it all slipping through his fingers so quickly. It was a funny feeling: he'd lived for almost two thousand years—1,999 to be exact—and all throughout the centuries, he'd never paid attention to the passing of time. He had taken it for granted. He had felt like he would live forever.

But now, with only weeks left to live, everything took on a supreme importance, a supreme urgency. Finally, after so many years on this earth, he felt what it was like to be mortal. To be human. To be frail, vulnerable. It was awful, like a cruel joke. Finally, he realized what humans went through. He couldn't understand how they dealt with it, how they lived with their own death sentence every day. It made him admire them more than he'd ever did.

He, like his entire clan, had known for centuries that there was an end-time to their existence. He'd always assumed that when the time came, he would deal with it gracefully, would have had enough of life, would be tired of all the centuries, of all the people coming and going. But now that the end was here, he wanted more time. It still wasn't enough.

Being an Immortalist, Sage's life was almost identical to that of a human's: he ate and drank and slept and woke and gained energy from food and drink—just like any other human. The only difference was, he could not die. If he did not eat or drink, he would not die from starvation; if he got injured, he would heal almost instantly. He could not get sick, or disease.

Luckily, his kind did not need to prey on humans, or animals—or anything—to sustain its life energy. They could co-habit with them peacefully. There were some among his clan who attacked humans for sport, for a drug-like high: if they chose to, late at night they could transform to an enormous raven-like creature, roam the skies, swoop down and wrap a human in an embrace with their huge, air-tight wings, holding them like that for minutes until they depleted all the human's psychic and emotional energy. They would leave them crumpled on the ground, collapsed, when they were through. They would never actually bite them. But they didn't need to—when they wrapped their wings tight around a human, it drew out all the energy they needed.

Of course, this was completely unnecessary for an Immortalist's existence. Those of his clan who did this did it for a high that only lasted for a few hours and sent them crashing after that. Sage could only always tell when one of his clan had fed—he could see it in the brightness of their eyes, the flush of their cheeks. Human-feeding was an unnecessary and hedonistic sport. It was also cruel, as it left the human victim psychotic. For this reason the Grand Council had outlawed human-feeding centuries ago. None of his immediate clan partook. After all, who wanted to draw so much negative attention?

But lately, things were starting to change. With only a few weeks left to live, he noticed his people acting differently. They were all on edge, acting desperate, and doing things they never would. He'd even heard that last night, one of his own had attacked a human.

Of course, he knew who it had to be: Lore. Who else? A distant cousin, Lore was the bad-apple of his clan, and had been a thorn in Sage's side for centuries. He was an energy addict, and he relished in causing trouble for his clan everywhere they went. He was also a hot-head, vindictive, and totally unpredictable.

Sage continued down the driveway, approaching their ancestral home—a huge, sprawling marble mansion surrounded by dozens of acres, right on the river. They had homes all over the world, of course; they had grand castles, and marble townhomes, and fortresses, and entire islands. But of all the homes around the world, Sage liked this one the most. Tucked away, far from any main roads, nestled against the tranquil Hudson River, this one felt most like home. He loved to sit out on the balcony, especially late at night, under the moon, and watch the reflection of the water. It made him feel as if he were the only one left in the world. He remembered, centuries ago, during the Revolutionary war, sitting out and watching the battles on the Hudson.

But now, as he walked towards the house, instead of being filled with joy, he was filled with dread. His clan had only recently moved back here, and in Sage's view, it was an act of desperation. He wanted to live out his remaining time in peace. Instead, the clan had raced back here, hoping, as always, to find a cure for their sickness, to prolong their lifetime. Sage knew it was ridiculous, a futile endeavor: they had been searching for a cure for as long as he could remember—and never, not once, not in any remote corner of the world, had they found it. They were all false leads, dead-ends. In his view, the cure was just a myth, a legend. There was no way to extend their lifetime. It would end, and that would be all. Sage was resigned to it. He just wanted to live out his life and enjoy what he had, instead of desperately chasing myths and fables.

But others in his clan felt differently. Especially his parents. Once again, they claimed to have sensed the last remaining vampire on earth, the mythical teenage girl rumored to hold the key to the cure. Sage had heard this before—many times. But this time, they were serious. They had moved everyone back here in hopes of finding her—and worse, they had assigned Sage to be the one to gain her trust. To find out if she held the key—and to make sure she gave it to him. Because legend had it that the key must be given freely, and could not be simply taken.

What bothered Sage most about all this was that, even if all of this was true, even if this was the right girl, even if she did hold the key, even if he managed to gain her trust and get the key—there was still the next part. Because in order for the cure to work, the vampire girl who gave it had to be killed. The thought of it repulsed Sage. He had never killed a soul—not in two thousand years—and he didn't plan on starting now. Especially a teenage girl.

As he thought of the girl he'd seen in the cafeteria today, Scarlet, it made him feel even sicker. She was the most beautiful girl he had ever seen, and the thought of her sent butterflies to his stomach. He felt awful having to be assigned to gain her trust, to find out her secrets—to potentially kill her. It was against everything he stood for. He would keep up appearances to please his parents and his clan—but he already knew that he would sooner kill himself than harm her.

What troubled him most was that, when he saw her, for the first time in his entire existence, he actually sensed something unusual: he felt he was in the presence of another immortal being. He knew right away that she was not one of his. Which meant she could only be one thing: a vampire. The last remaining vampire on earth.

The thought sent a shiver up his spine. Despite everything, he feared his clan had found her after all, and that the legend was real. Which meant a cure might be out there. Why now? With just a few weeks left to go? Of course, he wanted to live, just like all of them. But he would never want to live at the expense of someone else. Especially at *her* expense.

As Sage opened the huge, arched front door, he was greeted by a host of activity: as usual, his clan members loafed around the place, spread out in the grand room, sitting in chairs and couches, reading ancient leather-bound books, or ambling about and strolling on the patio. He'd lost count of how many cousins he had, but he knew at least a dozen of them had come back with them to this sprawling mansion. Being an Immortalist had its advantages, and time had been kind to them: none of them looked older than 18. A mix of boys and girls, while they were all close to 2,000 years old, like him, one would never know it. They were all gorgeous—with perfect, sculpted faces, flawless, looking as if they could grace covers of magazines. Some were dressed in the latest fashions—tight-fitting jeans, slim leather jackets—while others wore more regal, traditional outfits from other centuries—like long, black velvet cloaks with high collars. They all looked fashionable, and it was like walking into a modeling shoot.

Sage scanned the room, looking for any sign of Lore. It was their first day back here, and he couldn't believe Lore already had the audacity to go out and sap a human. Already, Sage's presence here was compromised; Lore had managed to cause trouble, to make life harder for him, to make them even more conspicuous in this town.

He looked carefully but saw no sign of him—he was probably off on his drug high. Probably lying on the roof, if he knew him.

"Mom and Dad want to see you," suddenly came a voice.

Sage turned and saw walking past him, his older sister, Phoenicia. With long, straight, jet black hair and wide black eyes, she looked nothing like Sage. She acted nothing like him, either. She could be competitive, jealous and territorial. Throughout the centuries, the two of them had a complicated relationship, often fraught with tension. Sage felt that she was always in competition with him, always trying to get their parents' attention, to shine more than he did. That was fine with Sage—he could care less about his parents' attention—but nonetheless, they always seemed to favor him, and that drove her crazy. She let it out on him. She seemed perpetually mad at him, and nothing seemed to change it.

She could also be controlling and manipulative. He never knew what to expect around her, and often felt as if he had to walk on eggshells. But at the same time, sometimes she could surprise him and be unexpectedly sweet and vulnerable, totally catching him off guard. Sometimes she even confided in him. He never knew what to expect.

"I watched you at school today," she reported.

He was shocked; he'd had no idea she'd been spying on him. He wondered if she did it on her own, or if her parents had planted her as a spy, to keep track of him.

"You didn't even try to talk to her. I told Mom and Dad, and they're really pissed. Brace yourself," she said, as she hurried off.

"Thanks," he answered. "Knew I could always count on you to put in a good word."

It was just like her, causing friction between him and his parents already. Already ratting him out. His face turned red with frustration. He resented her, and he resented his parents. He wasn't sure who he resented more. Not because they were all breathing down his neck and forcing him to.

Sage hurried through the vast, cavernous rooms of the mansion, through an arched door, down an endless corridor, across a bare room with wide-plank wood floors, up a wide, marble staircase, and finally, to a set of arched, double doors. His parents' study.

He knocked three times, and waited.

"Come in," came his Dad's muted voice. He could already sense that he was unhappy. He braced himself as he entered.

Seated behind the wide desk were his dad and mom. They both sat in high-backed leather chairs, staring back coldly. They did not look happy. Clearly, they had expected Sage to come running home from school and report to them right away. He could sense how impatient they were, on-edge. The end of their lifespan was getting to them, too. They had no time to waste, and they were mad because he'd wasted a precious day.

They were right. He had not rushed home. He had not even taken his car today, but had chosen to walk. He'd ambled about the school grounds, walked through the town, then took a long walk, slowly, back home. He wanted time to think, to process it all, to sort out his feelings for this girl. What he felt terrified him. It was a sense of a deep connection, a deep love towards her.

Why now? he wondered. *Why now, with only a few weeks left to live? When there was no time for their love to blossom? Why had he had to meet her now? Why couldn't they have met centuries before?*

"Why the delay?" his dad asked, wasting no time.

"Close the door," his mom snapped. Clearly, neither of them were in the mood for pleasantries.

Sage closed the door behind him, running through potential responses in his head. He resented, after all these centuries, still having to answer to them. Somehow it seemed to be a necessary evil, just part of the way things worked. It was especially unsettling because, they, being Immortalists, looked to be his own age, hardly older than 18.

He crossed the room and sat across from them. He felt like he was a little kid again, and hated it. He considered possible responses, and decided it was best, for now, just to set them at ease.

"I'm sorry," he said.

They stared back, not bothering to respond.

"You're on a mission," his dad reminded sternly. "We have no time. Are you not aware of that?"

"I am aware."

"So why the delay?" retorted his mom, impatient.

"I lost track of time," he lied.

His mother shook her head.

"Just like your sister. A dreamer. You still don't realize, do you? In a few weeks, you'll be dead. We'll *all* be dead. Does that mean nothing to you?"

"I did that which you asked of me," he replied. "I went there. I was in the school. I saw her."

"And?" his father prodded.

He paused.

"I did not have a chance to speak with her yet," he said.

His parents both sat up in their chairs, outraged. They were about to speak, but he cut them off.

"It was a crowded school," Sage said. "She was surrounded by friends. There was no way to approach her in an inconspicuous way. She was not alone for a second. I'm sorry. Perhaps tomorrow there will be more opportunity."

His father slowly shook his head, looking disappointed.

"I knew we made a mistake choosing your for this task. It is just as it always has been. Excuses. Delays. Don't you understand!?" he suddenly screamed. "This is not a mission of pleasantries! It is one of urgency!" he slammed his fist into the desk, rattling the china cup on it.

A tense silence fell over the room. Sage wanted to yell back, but thought it best to keep calm for now. If he wanted to save Scarlet, he had to stay calm and divert attention away from her.

"I'm not convinced she is the one, anyway," Sage said. "I feel confident that, once again, you're wasting your time," he lied.

"That is for us to decide," hissed his mother, "not you."

She suddenly jumped up from her chair and paced the room, looking distraught.

"If you can't complete this task, then we'll choose someone else who can. You have plenty of attractive cousins who would be more than happy to finish the job."

"Yes, you have many to choose from who could kill her quite easily," Sage said. "But how many do you have who could gain her confidence? Who can get her to willingly offer the key? After all, the key can't be taken. And killing her without the key is useless, isn't it? So you need me. You know that you do."

He knew he had them. After all, he was right: he'd always been known for his tact, his ability to gain trust and confidence. That was because he was sincere. None of his cousins had that trait.

77

"If she's not the one, as you predict," his father said, "then it doesn't matter either way, does it? In that case, we might as well just kill her. Maybe I should just send Lore to take care of it now?"

Sage reddened at his bluff being called.

"What would you gain by that?" Sage asked, on thin ice.

"What do you care?" smiled back his father. "Unless you have some reason to protect her?"

Sage fumed. As usual, they had caught him, had managed to back him into a corner. He had to think quick. He cleared his throat.

"All I'm saying," he began, "is give me another day. Surely one more day is not a lot to ask for. These things take time. I will fulfill the mission. I will discover her secrets. And if she is the one, I will get her to give me the key."

"And then, we will kill her," his mother added.

He glared back at her, his eyes darkening. He'd had enough.

"You will get your way, mother," he said back in a steely tone. "After all, you always have, haven't you? But what if this trick doesn't work. What if, like the rest of us, you'll die in a few weeks? Then what, mother? Then who will you have left to order around?"

With that, Sage stood, turned, and strutted from the room.

"Sage, get back here!" his father yelled after him.

But he'd had enough. He stormed out the room and slammed the door behind him. He couldn't stand to hear their voices for one more moment.

As he closed the door behind him, he looked up and saw, standing there, his cousin. Lore. He was grinning back at him with an evil grin, his eyes glazed over in a drug haze. Lore was three inches taller than Sage, at six foot five, and had broad shoulders and a square jaw. He sneered down, dressed in his black leather jacket, unshaven, stubble on his face.

"Hello, cousin," he said.

It took all Sage's willpower to control his anger.

"Eavesdropping again?" Sage asked.

Lore only grinned wider.

"Your new mission. Is Scarlet her name?" his grin widened. "She sounds delightful. Don't worry, if you can't finish her off, I will."

Sage wanted to kill him right then and there, with his bare hands. But he couldn't.

,

78

So instead, he forced himself to walk away, bumping Lore's shoulder hard as he walked past him.

Sage needed to stay focused. More than anything, he needed to divert attention from this girl.

Because deep down, in his heart, he knew that Scarlet was the one. The key to his clan's survival.

And he would do everything in his power to save her.

CHAPTER ELEVEN

Scarlet came home from school feeling totally on edge. She kept reliving in her head that fateful moment in the cafeteria, when Blake was about to ask her to the dance and Vivian interrupted them. She was so mad just thinking about it. It seemed obvious that Blake liked her; but for some reason, he just didn't have the backbone to stand up to Vivian. It was like he was afraid to make her mad.

She hated that about Blake. She was totally obsessed with them, but she hated the fact that he didn't have the spine to stand up to her, to stand up for what he really wanted, despite what anybody else thought. Scarlet felt that she deserved a guy who wasn't afraid to express his feelings for her, in front of anyone, no matter what the consequences, who wasn't afraid to just walk up to her and ask her to the dance. Why was that so hard? Why did guys always have to deliberate, to hedge their bets? Why couldn't they just pick one girl and not think twice? Why did they always seem to keep their options open, always keep one eye on one other girl, just in case?

Scarlet fumed as she hurried up her steps, across the wide front porch, and entered her house. The late October weather was starting to pick up, the temperature dropping. A cold breeze had chased her all the way home from school, and it was nice and warm inside.

As she walked in, Ruth barked hysterically, whining and jumping on her, dancing around her in circles, so excited. As always, once she saw Ruth, all Scarlet's troubles faded into the background. She knelt down and gave her a big hug, kissing her all over her face.

The smell of warm food wafted through the house, and as Scarlet stood, she noticed the fire in the fireplace. She was beginning to feel at ease again. There was nothing she loved more than a fire, and the fact that there was one burning only meant one thing: daddy was home from work in time for dinner.

"First fire of the year!" Caleb announced as he marched into the room, a satisfied grin on his face, carrying a small bundle of logs and setting them down beside the mantel. "What do you think?" he asked, as he came over and gave her a hug.

She gave him a big hug, thrilled he was home. She loved her dad more than anything, and his presence was always so reassuring in her life.

"I'm surprised," she said. "You usually wait until Thanksgiving."

"I know," he answered. "But it got so cold, I figured why wait? After all, it's practically November."

"I love it," Scarlet said. "Can't come early enough for me."

Ruth seemed to feel the same, as she walked over to the fireplace and curled up in a ball a few feet away.

"How are you feeling?" Caleb asked, looking at her earnestly.

Scarlet hated when he looked at her like that, so worried. She didn't want anyone to worry about her. She started to make her way towards the dining room.

"I'm fine," she snapped, and immediately felt bad, sounding a little bit too edgy. "Don't worry about me. Really. It was just like the flu or whatever."

"I'm not worried about you," Caleb said. "I know that your fine. But your mother is worried."

Scarlet looked at him, suddenly realizing, and dreading seeing her mom. The last thing she wanted was a worry session right now.

"How's she doing?"

Caleb shrugged. "She's a bit shaken. You gave us a fright. But she'll be okay."

Scarlet's stomach dropped at the thought of the dinner ahead. She could already envision how worried her mom would be, and she really didn't want to be around it right now. Her mom had already texted her three times today to ask how she was. It was annoying. She appreciated how much her parents cared, but at the same time, it could be suffocating. She just wanted them to trust her, to trust that she was fine.

She hurried into the dining room, and as she did, Ruth jumped up and accompanied her.

The table was beautifully set, fresh flowers in the middle, and filled with food. A large roasted chicken sat in the center, and there were sides of mashed potatoes, stuffing, corn, green beans…. It looked like Thanksgiving. And it smelled delicious.

As Caleb entered behind her, suddenly her mom burst through the double doors, carrying a small bowl of gravy. She looked up and saw Scarlet and looked startled. Then she smiled back.

"Perfect timing," she said.

She set down the gravy and came over and stood before Scarlet, reaching up and brushing the hair out of her face, just like she used to do when Scarlet was a little girl.

"How are you feeling?" she asked earnestly. "I was so worried about you all day."

Scarlet just wanted this whole thing to go away. She really didn't want to dwell on it.

"I'm fine mom, really. Please don't worry about me."

Caitlin stared into her eyes, and Scarlet could see she was not convinced.

"Let's eat," Scarlet said, impatient, twisting out of her grip.

The three of them took their seats at the table, Caleb at the head, and Scarlet and Caitlin facing each other on either side of him, Ruth sitting by Scarlet's side. The first thing Scarlet did was reach out, grab a hunk of meat, and, when no one was looking, reach down and give it to Ruth. She knew her dad would get mad, so she did it stealthily.

But Ruth gave it away, smacking her lips loudly on the huge hunk of meat. Caleb looked down, then up at Scarlet.

"Scarlet," he said ominously, realizing.

"It was just a small piece—" she began.

"I just fed her," her dad said. "She's going to get fat."

"Sorry."

He let it go. He reached out and began serving portions onto her plate, then onto Caitlin's, then onto his own. Once her plate was filled, Scarlet reached up to take her first bite, when suddenly, her mom cleared her throat.

"I think that before we eat, we should all say grace together."

Scarlet looked at her dad, who looked back at her, equally astonished. They had never said grace once in their entire time together as a family.

What had gotten into her mom? Scarlet wondered.

Her dad slowly put down his fork, and Scarlet reluctantly put down hers. Her mom lowered her head, and Caleb did, too. Scarlet refused, annoyed. It was enough already. Clearly, this was about her being sick. Why couldn't her mom just move on?

"Dear Lord. Thank you for blessing us with this beautiful meal. Thank you for blessing us with such a beautiful family. And thank you for keeping us all safe and protected. Please continue to watch over us and keep us all healthy. Amen."

"Amen," Caleb replied.

Scarlet, still mad, feeling in the spotlight, didn't respond. After a long day of being in the spotlight at school, this was really the last thing she needed know. Instead, she sighed, reached up, and took her first bite. The food, at least, was delicious.

The three of them sat there in awkward silence, eating. At this point, Scarlet just wanted to get through dinner and get to her room and shut the door, shut out the world. She just wanted to go on Facebook and unwind. She was still reeling from her day.

As she ate, she couldn't stop thinking about the dance on Friday, and couldn't stop wondering if Blake had asked Vivian. Or, if not, if he would summon the courage to ask her tomorrow her, Scarlet, tomorrow. What would she do if he didn't ask her? Would she go alone? Not go at all? Should she take the initiative and ask Blake? No, she couldn't do that.

Throwing a major wrinkle in everything was the fact that, for some weird reason, she also couldn't stop thinking about the new kid she saw today. Sage. She kept thinking of that funny feeling she had when she saw him, when their eyes locked—like an electric jolt. It was unlike anything she had experienced before. She didn't understand it, and it freaked her out. Why was she even thinking about him? A part of her ached to see him again—and another part hoped that she would never see him again.

Scarlet was beginning to feel too worked up, overwhelmed by all the emotions swirling around within her. She was feeling anxious. She just wanted tomorrow to come already, wanted to get answers, resolution, to know what was going to happen.

"Scarlet?" came her mom's voice.

Scarlet looked up, jolted out of her thoughts.

"What's on your mind?"

Scarlet paused, wondering what, if anything to tell her.

"Nothing," she finally said. She really didn't want to talk about the dance, or Blake, or the new kid. Or anything. She just wanted the day to be over.

"How was school today?" her dad asked.

"Fine, I guess."

"Was it okay that you were late?"

She shrugged. "I only missed one class. It wasn't a big deal. I got the homework assignment. A few people asked what happened, but then they let it go. Anyway, no one really cared that much—they were too busy obsessing over Tina."

"Tina?" her dad asked.

"A girl in my grade. Apparently, she, like, went crazy last night or something."

Her dad looked at her mom in surprise, and she nodded back.

"I read about it in the paper this morning," she said, looking right at Scarlet. "Was she a close friend of yours?"

"I barely knew her," Scarlet answered.

"What happened?" her dad asked.

"Apparently, she like freaked out last night," Scarlet said. "Went crazy. She's like in the hospital or something."

"The papers said an animal attacked her," her mom added.

Her dad looked at her, eyes open wide.

"An animal?"

"That's what the paper said. But nobody really knows. It happened just a few blocks away."

As she said it, her mom looked at Scarlet, as if examining her, as if wondering something. It started to freak Scarlet out. Once again, Scarlet felt a pit in her stomach as she worried if maybe she had crossed paths with Tina that night. The timing of it was so weird. She looked back down at her food, just wanting to finish quick.

They all continued to eat in silence.

"I went to church today," her mom suddenly announced.

Scarlet stopped in mid-chew, stunned. She noticed her dad froze, too. They both exchanged a look.

Scarlet didn't even know how to respond. Church? She had never been in a church once in her life, and had never known her mom to go to one, either. She was beginning to seriously worry if her mom was losing it, having some kind of nervous breakdown. Had her being sick shaken her up that much? Or was something else going on with her?

"Why?" Scarlet asked, breaking the thick silence.

"I felt the need to talk to someone," she said, "about what happened yesterday. The thought of losing you..."

Her mom suddenly teared up, and wiped a tear from the corner of her eye.

Scarlet felt a pit in her stomach.

"Mom, I'm fine," she said, more edgy than she wanted to be. "Seriously. There's nothing wrong with me. God. Why are you making such a big deal of this?"

"I saw Father McMullen. Do you remember him? He remembers you. He met you, when you were a child."

"I don't remember ever even going to church," Scarlet said.

"When you were young, we took you a few times. Anyway, he said he wants to see you."

Scarlet looked at her mom as if she had two heads. Who was this person who had landed at their dinner table?

"He wants to meet me? Why? What are you talking about?"

"I told him about you, and about our family, and about what happened, and he thought it would be a good idea to meet you."

"Why?" Scarlet insisted, her voice rising. Now she was getting mad. What was her mom telling this priest about her?

"Caitlin, what are you talking about?" her dad interjected, setting down his fork.

"Is there anything so terrible about meeting with a priest?" she asked. "About going to church?"

"I'm *not* going to church," Scarlet said. "Hello, I haven't gone my entire life. Why should I start going now? Because I got sick? Because I disappeared for a few hours?"

"Scarlet," her mom said, "please. I'm asking you to do me a favor. I never ask anything of you. I'm only asking this one thing. Please. I'm worried about you. I want you to come to church with me. I want you to meet Father McMullen."

"What's the point?" Scarlet responded, feeling her heart pounding inside her chest. "I don't understand. Like I said, I'm fine."

Was her mom losing her mind? Was her family going crazy?

"You don't know that," her mom said.

"What are you saying: I'm not fine?"

Scarlet felt herself shaking inside.

"Caitlin, Scarlet is fine," her dad interjected. She was grateful that at least he was taking her side. "Just because the event shook you—"

"I just want her to meet with the priest," she responded, her voice rising, too, more insistent than ever. "Please. Just do this for me. He can heal you."

Scarlet found herself standing, her face flushing red.

"Heal me of *what*?" she snapped, nearly shouting.

Her mom just stared back, silent.

"You're crazy!" she yelled back at her mom. "You're losing it! *You're* the one that needs to be healed! Seriously. *You* go talk to someone. Like a shrink or something. I don't need to be healed. I'm fine. I'm sorry if you see me as some kind of freak. But I'm not. I'm perfectly normal!" she shouted, as if trying to convince herself, too.

Scarlet burst into tears as she turned and fled the room, running up the steps, crying, Ruth at her heels.

She could hardly process it all. She couldn't believe that her mom thought of her as a sick person. As needing to see a priest. To be healed. What did that even mean? What did she think was wrong with her?

As Scarlet ran up the steps she heard her parents voices below, arguing with each other. She heard her dad sticking up for her, yelling at her mom, and heard her mom yelling back. Scarlet cried harder. She felt as if her entire family life was crumbling around her. Was she to blame? What was going on? It seemed like just yesterday everything was so perfect.

Scarlet ran down the hall and slammed her bedroom door behind her. She heard her mom's footsteps on the staircase, then down the hall, coming towards her door.

"Scarlet, I want talk to you!" her mom shouted, outside her door.

"Go away!" she screamed back.

"Scarlet, please, open the door!"

But Scarlet ignored it. She locked her door, crossed her room, and curled up in her favorite chair, Ruth at her lap.

Scarlet sat there, never feeling more alone in the world, as she cried and cried. After a long time, finally, her mom's voice disappeared from the door.

Scarlet eventually sat up, wiped away her tears, and reached over and grabbed her small, white leather journal from her end table. She used to write in it every night, though she hadn't written in a while. Now, she felt the need to. She had to make sense of her world, to get a hold on her range of conflicting emotions.

She pulled back the cover, flipped through the pages and found an empty page. She reached over and grabbed her favorite, purple pen, then leaned over and began to write:

Today was the worst day. I woke up in the hospital. I can hardly believe it. It was so weird. I came home sick, then blacked out, and I don't remember anything in between. Mom and Dad say I ran out the house, and that I was missing for a while. Which really freaks me out. I don't remember it at all. I really want to know where I went. What I did. If I saw any of my friends. Hopefully, no one saw me.

I'm also freaked about what happened to me. Am I sick? Was it sleepwalking or something? Will it happen again? Mom doesn't want to let it go. She keeps asking me if I'm okay, and she's so worried. Now she wants me to talk to a priest. It's so annoying. I can't stand to be around her right now, and I've never really felt this way before.

The dance on Friday is causing me so much pressure. I was sure Blake would ask me today. I'm sure he would have if it weren't for Vivian. I hate her. Every time Blake gets near me, I feel she's waiting to steal him. I don't know if he asked her. Or if he'll ask me. I hate dances. This is all so stupid anyway.

I wish I knew where Blake stood. We had a really good time the other night, at the movies, on my birthday. I really want to be close to him. I want him to be my boyfriend. I don't really know if he feels the same. Is he not into me? Is he into Vivian? Did I do something wrong?

Then there's this new kid. Sage. The one Maria likes. It was so weird, seeing him today. I can't explain it. It's like I knew him. I wish I hadn't seen him. He's Maria's territory after all, and I'm into Blake. Or am I? I don't really understand how I'm feeling—and that bothers me more than anything.

I need answers. Tomorrow can't come soon enough.

CHAPTER TWELVE

The next day for Scarlet came and went too fast. She rushed off to school, leaving early so she didn't have to deal with her parents, and her morning classes had gone by in a whirl. She'd had no contact with Blake whatsoever, and had hardly even seen him. She caught a glimpse of him in the halls, as she rushed from one class to the next. She hadn't seen that new kid, Sage. And she hadn't seen Vivian either. It was just a long and boring and anxiety-provoking day, keeping her in suspense as the minutes ticked slowly from class to class.

She'd been so nervous for lunchtime, expecting to see them all in the cafeteria, expecting Blake to come up to her. But her stupid science teacher had kept her after class, and by the time she reached the cafeteria, she only had a few minutes to eat, and had missed everybody. She was so mad at her teacher. She was sure that if she'd arrived just a few minutes earlier she would've run into Blake, and he would've asked her.

Now, the day was almost over, with only a few periods left, as Scarlet walked with Maria down the halls, heading towards gym and the playing fields. They walked outside into the beautiful October day, the sun shining everywhere, lighting up the leaves in a million colors, and she headed eagerly with Maria across the acres of grass. At least she was sure that this time, she would see Blake. They all had gym together, after all. Several classes met for gym—nearly a hundred kids—but still, there was no way he could really avoid her—unless he wanted to.

At least, finally, she would know how he really felt. If it turned out that he didn't want to take her to the dance, fine—she could at least get clear in her head that she would either go with someone else, or not go at all, and be able to stop obsessing over this.

"Think we'll get picked for the same team?" Maria asked, as they jogged towards the big crowd of kids.

"Hope so."

Scarlet wasn't exactly the best athlete on the field. She wasn't the most coordinated person in the world, and she never got picked first, or close to first. She just wasn't as competitive as some of the other girls. The gym teacher always let them divide into teams and pick whoever they wanted; Scarlet just hoped that she got picked on Maria's team.

Scarlet jogged with Maria across the grass, and it felt good to be out of school and under the open sky, as they headed towards the crowd. As they went, Scarlet scanned the fields, looking for Blake. She spotted him in the distance, on the adjacent field, with the boys as they divvied up teams for the boys' football game. But he wasn't looking her way and there was no way to really talk to him. She would just have to hope he came over after the game.

"OMG, he's here," Maria suddenly said in an excited whisper. "I can't believe it. Don't look but I think he's staring at me."

At first Scarlet was confused, but then she looked in the other direction, and spotted someone else: Sage. She did a double take. There he stood, hands in his jacket pockets, standing alone on the sidelines, watching. She couldn't believe it. He was here. And he was looking right at her.

She found herself mesmerized by the sight of him, and had to look away.

"I'm dying," Maria said. "Is he still watching me?"

Scarlet tried to think of how to phrase it without hurting her feelings.

"Um…I can't really tell," she said.

As they walked through the throngs of girls and saw who was out on the field today, Scarlet felt a sense of dread. Of course. There was Vivian, already warming up, practicing her soccer skills, kicking it deftly back and forth between all of her friends. All of the popular girls seemed to be not only cheerleaders, but expert soccer players; somehow it was Scarlet's fate to always be at their mercy to get picked, as one of the popular girls was inevitably in charge of the picking.

The coach suddenly blew a whistle and the girls huddled around, preparing to be picked.

"Vivian and Doris are team captains today. They'll pick," the coach announced.

Of course, Scarlet thought.

The picking began, and of the group of about twenty girls, Scarlet was picked close to last. Of course, she was picked by Doris, not Vivian. But luckily, at least Doris chose Maria to be on her team, too.

The coach blew another whistle, and Scarlet ran out to the field with the other girls, who were all screaming and yelling as the soccer ball was put into play. They all raced back and forth, kicking the ball to each other, passing expertly. Scarlet was distracted, looking over and catching a glance of Sage. He was still looking at her. At her, and no one else.

Scarlet forced herself to look away, to concentrate. She hardly knew what to make of it.

She hurried to catch up to the action, but found herself a bit winded, not in the best of shape. Moments later, though, the ball broke free from the pack, and to Scarlet's surprise, it went flying right for her. Her heart started pounding. This had never happened before, and she hardly knew what to do.

She started kicking the ball down field, running alongside it. There was no one near here, and she, amazingly, soon found herself in range of the goal. She felt her heart race, as she might actually get her first chance ever to even attempt a goal.

"Go Scarlet go!" Maria encouraged behind her.

The goal was in sight, and there was no one between her and the goalie.

Scarlet took a few more steps and geared up to kick.

Suddenly, she felt a sharp cleat dig into her ankle, felt her foot kicked out from under her, and landed hard on the grass.

"That was such a foul!" screamed Maria to the coach. But he ignored it, as he let the game continue.

Scarlet looked up to see Vivian standing over her, smirking down.

"Sorry," she said sarcastically. "Must've thought you were the ball."

Vivian, smiling, high-fived one of her friends, and raced back downfield with the others.

Maria held out a hand for Scarlet and she took it. She got up slowly, disoriented, her ankle in pain, and her side hurting from the fall. Most of all, she was embarrassed: she hoped that Sage hadn't witnessed that.

"God, I hate her," Maria said. "That was so wrong. She totally robbed you of that goal. I'm gonna get her back."

As Scarlet stood there, fuming with the indignity of it all, she suddenly started to experience something she never had before. She began to feel something burn up inside her, rise up from within. A sense of outrage and injustice burned inside her, and she began to feel a heat rising through her veins. She could feel the sensation tingling in her arms; it almost felt as if the veins were popping out of her skin.

For the first time in her life, she felt a burning desire for revenge. Her anger burned, grew stronger and stronger, as she felt a surge of energy race through her. A superhuman strength. In that moment, she felt she was capable of anything.

"No," Scarlet said, taken aback by the strength in her own voice. "I got this."

Scarlet suddenly raced down the field, running right for Vivian. Vivian was a good fifty yards away, but something was happening to Scarlet, and she found herself able to zoom in on her, in crystal-clear detail. She had never had vision like this before.

Or speed like this. As she ran, it was as if her legs ran for her. It was as if everyone else was running in slow motion, as if she were a gazelle among kids. In just moments she covered the entire field and was closing in directly on Vivian.

Vivian, of course, had the ball, and was moving it downfield. And she never saw Scarlet coming.

Scarlet kicked the ball out from under her, drove it further downfield, then turned around, all in the flash of an eye, and about ten yards away, kicked it hard, right at Vivian.

The ball went flying in a line drive, and hit Vivian right in the stomach. She keeled over, on the grass, clutching her stomach, as the coach blew the whistle.

Several girls came running over to Vivian, helping her up, making sure she was okay. Vivian got to her feet, fine but embarrassed. She glared at Scarlet with a look of death.

Scarlet stood there and smiled back, feeling vindicated.

"You little witch," Vivian said threateningly.

She approached, but now, Scarlet was completely unafraid. On the contrary, she felt a power unlike any she'd ever known, and welcomed the confrontation.

Vivian lunged at Scarlet, claws out, aiming right for her face. But before she could get close, several of her friends grabbed her from behind, pulling her back.

"Vivian, it's not worth it," her friend said.

More girls got between them, and slowly, reluctantly, Vivian backed away.

"You're dead," Vivian yelled, pointing at her.

Scarlet looked over to the sidelines, and saw Sage still there, watching her. Now, he had a small smile on his face.

The coach blew the whistle, and again the ball was put into play. One of Vivian's friends managed to get it, and instead of moving it downfield, she passed it to Vivian, setting her up.

Vivian turned away from the goal and instead prepared to kick it directly at Scarlet.

But Scarlet, with her new reflexes, sensed it coming. As Vivian geared up to kick it at her, about ten yards away, Scarlet burst into action. With lightning speed, she raced for the ball and reached it before Vivian could even finish winding back her leg. She stole it right out from under her and ran with it downfield. Vivian kicked at nothing but air, and her leg went flying up and she fell right on her butt, humiliated.

By then, Scarlet was already far downfield. There was no one who could get within ten yards of her as she zigzagged between everyone deftly. Soon, it was just her and the goalie—and the goalie didn't stand a chance. Scarlet wound up and kicked the ball so hard, it went past the goalie and into the net with force enough to lift the entire goal and send it crashing back, it's metal frame crashing to the ground.

Everyone stood there frozen, hardly believing what they just witnessed.

"OMG, Scarlet?" Maria said as she came running up to her. "That was like—amazing. Like unreal. How did you do that?"

Scarlet stood there, hardly registering what had just happened. She'd been so caught up in the moment, she hardly understood it herself.

The coach blew the whistle and screamed out. "Gym is over! Everyone back to class!"

The other girls filtered off the field slowly, giving Scarlet amazed looks.

"Nice kick, Scarlet," a girl said admiringly.

"Yeah, nice kick weirdo freak," came a snotty comment from one of the popular girls, as the group of them brushed passed her.

But Vivian now looked at Scarlet with something like fear, and she kept her distance, clustering with her friends. She glared at her, but this time she didn't dare come anywhere near her. Scarlet realized, with satisfaction, that she must have shook them. Finally, she felt vindicated. Even if they did think she was a freak.

"OMG, he's staring at me again," came Maria's voice.

Scarlet turned and followed Maria's glance to the sidelines. There stood Sage, hands still in his pockets, a smile on his face, staring right at Scarlet.

"Am I imagining it, or is he really looking at me?" Maria asked.

Scarlet hardly knew what to say. As she stared back into his eyes, she found herself mesmerized, unable to look away.

"OMG, he's coming over here!" Maria announced, and turned away, blushing. "Like, what do I say?"

Scarlet noticed it, too. He began to walk in their direction, and as he did, staring right at her all the while, she felt her heart begin to pound.

"Hey, nice goal!" suddenly came a voice from behind her.

Scarlet turned to see Blake standing there, holding a football, with two of his buddies, cheeks flushed.

Scarlet was overwhelmed—it was too much going on at once. She hardly knew which direction to turn. She looked back, over her shoulder, for Sage.

But when she turned, he was gone.

She was amazed. She didn't know how it was possible. How could Sage have disappeared like that? There were nothing but open fields all around them, and nowhere to hide. How could he have just vanished?

Scarlet was mad at Blake for scaring him away.

Damn it, why had it all have to happen at once?

"Um…thanks," she said, flustered.

"Anyway, like, a few us thought we'd cut for the day. Head down to the lake. You guys like, want to join?"

Scarlet was taken aback. She hadn't expected this. She didn't really know Blake's friends well, and doubted Maria would want to go, since she never missed class. She was nervous at the idea of missing class, and of going herself—but she was more worried that if she said no, it would be like rejecting Blake. Wouldn't that seal her fate for the dance?

"You mean cut class?" Maria asked, disapprovingly. "Like the rest of the day?"

"It's no big deal," one of Blake's friend said. "There's only a few classes left."

"Well, I have a quiz next period," Maria said. "I can't. And we don't cut class."

"Whoa," Blake's friend said back, mocking her. "Excuse me. Goody-goody."

"Come on Scarlet, let's go," Maria said, grabbing her wrist.

"I think it's a great idea," came a voice over Scarlet's shoulder. "We'd love to go."

Scarlet cringed. She looked and saw Vivian standing there, with two of her popular friends, grinning back at Blake. Blake's friends lit up at the sight of them.

"Awesome," two of them said.

Blake himself looked unsure. After all, he'd invited Scarlet, hadn't he? How dare Vivian come over and pretend like *she* was the one invited.

"Let's go, Scarlet," Maria said.

Scarlet stood there, torn. She didn't want to cut class. That wasn't her. At the same time, the thought of Blake hanging out with Vivian made her sick. This was her chance. After all, the dance was Friday. And if there was any chance of Blake's asking her, she felt she had to do this.

"I'll come," she said to Blake.

Blake broke into a smile.

"Scarlet, seriously?" Maria said. "Your parents would kill you."

Scarlet turned to her.

"It'll be fine. Like they said, the day's basically over anyway. Come with me."

But Maria shook her head and stormed off without another word, clearly pissed.

Scarlet watched Maria leave. That left Scarlet all alone, with Blake and his friends—and Vivian, and these popular girls. The thought of it churned her stomach. But she felt like she had no choice. She had to do what she had to do.

When Scarlet turned back around, the group was already several feet away, their backs to her, walking quickly across the fields, down towards the woods. Vivian, she noticed, had already stepped-up and locked Blake's arms in one of hers, yanking him close to her, as they strutted off.

Scarlet swallowed hard. This was not going to be easy.

CHAPTER THIRTEEN

Caitlin sat in her office in the university library, elbow on her desk, head in her palm, poring over the book before her. She had spent all morning pulling rare books from the stacks, and now her desk was covered with them.

But these were not the usual books she worked on. When she'd arrived this morning, the first thing she had done was clear her desk of all her work books—and made room for a whole new set of books. She had walked into work today determined, obsessed with finding out exactly what was happening to her daughter and figuring out how to help her.

After her horrible argument with Scarlet the night before—the first argument she could ever remember the two of them having—Caitlin had a terrible night, tossing and turning with little sleep. She kept thinking of Father McMullen, of their meeting. She recalled the look her husband and daughter had given her when she'd asked Scarlet to come to church. Caitlin couldn't help feeling that her own family now hated and distrusted her.

Caitlin felt increasingly alone, and more and more she wondered if she was losing her mind, imagining the whole thing. She desperately needed to find proof that she was right. That she was not crazy.

Caitlin had awakened determined to take action, and had figured the perfect plan, had realized at least one thing that she could do. She could use her expertise. She could go back to work and use all the library's resources, read up on anything and everything related to vampirism. She could learn about its history, its origins, its rituals, and anything and everything even peripherally related to it, including all forms of magic and sorcery and occultism.

Caitlin had entered the library at seven AM, an hour before it opened, and had let herself in. She had walked down the empty lobby with a newfound energy, determined to use all her skills to understand and decode what was happening to Scarlet. Whether it was myth or fact, civilization had been recording vampire legends and stories for thousands of years, and surely, all the collective knowledge and wisdom of thousands of years had to contain *something* that could be of help to her.

Caitlin had crossed the corridors of the university's ultra-modern library, the walls a sleek modern white, her shoes echoing on the marble floor beneath her. She'd felt a bit creepy walking through this huge empty structure, the only one in the building, but had put it out of her mind as she'd hurried up the steps, her shoes clicking as she went, and quickly lost herself in the stacks.

Luckily her library had a reputation for its vast collection of rare volumes, which is what had lured her to accept a job here. They also had a constant traveling exhibit, books on loan from other universities and collections; as fate would have it, October was "Occult Month," and they had several additional volumes on loan that they normally didn't—some of the rarest in the world, in fact.

Before Caitlin hit the stacks, she'd used their online catalogue system, doing her research, using her brilliant mind to immediately get an overview of the rarest and most important volumes in the field. Once she immersed herself in a topic like this, she could take it all in with dazzling speed, process and analyze it faster than just about anyone. As she expected, there were a lot of dubious and skeptical books in the occult genre—books that sounded hokey or were dismissed by scholars. But there were a handful of titles that seemed to persist throughout the centuries, embraced by one generation after the next, and which even scholars could not dismiss so easily. Within an hour, she felt confident she had an overview of the dozen or so most important books in the field that she had to read.

As she searched the catalog, she was thrilled to see her library had, on hand, editions of most of them

Caitlin grabbed a cart and had dove into the stacks, looking up each book by its call number, and slowly adding them to her stack. Some of the books were harder to find than others, and she'd had to use a ladder and go to the top, dusty shelf, deeper in the stacks than she'd ever been. One book she found stuck between two books, and literally had to pry it out. Another book she couldn't find anywhere—until she realized that it was on display in the front window, for the Occult Exhibit; she guiltily unlocked the glass, slid it back, reached in, and removed it, making a mental note to replace it as soon as possible, before anybody noticed.

She was beginning to feel a little better, a little more in control, as she filled her cart to overflowing, with 15 leather-bound books on the subject. Satisfied, she'd wheeled it back to her desk, cleared her other books, and covered it with these.

That was hours ago. It was after lunchtime, now, and Caitlin had not stopped reading for a second. Her back and joints were stiff, her eyes were hurting from the non-stop reading, and she had already sneezed way too many times from the dust.

The book she was reading now was a huge, oversized volume with thick leather binding, cracked along the spine. It probably weighed ten pounds, and was at least twelve inches wide and long. She had it opened to the middle of the book, and each page she turned crackled with age. The pages were thick, so much thicker than those of modern books, and yellow with age. It was a physically gorgeous volume, published in 1661, interspersed with hand-drawn illustrations, some of them in color. Caitlin turned the pages with the utmost care as she went, not wanting to deface it in any way.

Thus far her marathon reading session had been interesting, but she hadn't found anything compelling enough to convince her. She read volumes on vampirism and occultism and witches and magic and spells, and now, she was deep into a treatise on demonology. It amazed her that for thousands of years, myths and legends of vampires had persisted, in every language, and every country. Amazingly, the entire world had its own vampire tales.

How was it possible? she wondered. Dozens of cultures and languages and countries, all with their own, independent, vampire stories? From the remotest corners of Africa, to the far corners of Russia—places and times where people had no way of communicating with each other—yet still, documenting the same exact stories. She was starting to feel convinced that vampirism was real. Otherwise, how else could one explain it? It would have to be a huge coincidence.

Many of the vampire legends seemed to have a common theme: a vampire was created when someone died in a disturbing way, for example by murder, suicide, or disease—or when someone died a sudden, unexpected death. This was especially the case if the person was a low soul, such as a murderer or thief. Many of the stories had the vampire buried by the local villagers, only to have them visit the grave the next day and see it disrupted, the soil freshly overturned, the body still intact, not decomposing. In some stories, the corpse rose from the grave and attacked people; in others it stayed put, but the spirit of the deceased visited family and friends at night and tormented them. In many stories, the only way to kill the vampire was to drive a stake through its heart. But in older stories they did not use stakes—rather, they killed vampires before they could arise by burying corpses with bricks in their mouth, since they believed that evil spirits could enter a corpse through an open mouth.

Caitlin found herself getting lost, deeper and deeper in the world of vampire mythology and fables. It was becoming harder and harder for her to separate what was real from fantasy. Nonetheless, the more she read, the more she felt validated, certain that there was something real to all this. She felt connected to history, to the centuries. Other people had experienced this before. It was not just her.

But she did not find what she was looking for. She didn't know exactly what it was she needed to find, but she imagined that maybe it was some sort of ritual, or remedy, or ceremony, or service—something tangible and concrete that could help Scarlet. Transform her back to human. Something in the literature that explicitly stated that there was a way to cure vampirism. To bring the afflicted back to normal.

But so far, she found nothing. The only thing close were the ways to stop a vampire for all time—to kill them for good. Sometimes, this was accompanied by an ancient funeral service. In fact, they would repeat the funeral service, three times, and that would put the vampire to rest for all time. Oddly, as Caitlin read that, she felt some sort of memory, some sort of connection to that. But she didn't understand what.

But this was not what Caitlin wanted: she needed to heal Scarlet, not kill her.

As she finished yet another book and slid it aside, with still no mention of healing anywhere, she began to feel a sense of despair.

She lifted the final book on the stack, a small, leather-bound volume with a red spine, entitled *De Fascino Libri Tres* by Leonardo Vairo. Caitlin summoned her knowledge of Latin, and knew that translated to: *Three Books of Charms, Spells and Sorceries.*

Intrigued, she turned the cover, and saw that it was all in Latin. Luckily, her Latin was still good enough for her to translate in her head. The long title page read: "In which all the species and causes of spells are described and explained with the Philosophers and

Theologians. With the ways to fight the illusions of Demons, and the refutation of the causes behind the power of Witchcraft. 1589. Venice."

Caitlin dove into the book, scanning through, turning the pages as fast as she could, looking for any mention of vampires, of how to heal or cure one, how to bring one back to normal life.

As she began to read, she suddenly slowed down. She went back and read it again. Then again. Her heart started beating with hope. She could tell right away that this book was very different than the others. This, of all the books, felt the most real to her, the most scholarly, the most impartial. It wasn't filled with hyperbole and myth and wild stories told by grandmothers. This one was written, paradoxically, by a bishop, in the 16th century. Also a doctor, he had seen dozens of inexplicable cases of corpses coming back to life—and of people transforming into vampires. He wrote with such medical detail, had documented every case so fastidiously, that Caitlin felt this volume was authentic.

As she kept reading, her hands trembling with excitement, she came across something that struck her as pure gold:

"It was not until the late spring, long after the ground had thawed, that I stumbled across something that put an end to our small village's epidemic. It was a combination of certain herbs. When used in conjunction with the ritual, it healed the vampire before my eyes. She went from hysterical, desperately seeking blood, hardly able to be chained to her bed, to the teenager we all once knew. As of this writing, many years later, she never returned to vampirism and remains in her perfect state. The remedy only works if the vampire in question has not yet fed, has not yet inflicted pain on a human being. Thus it is imperative that one catch the vampire in the early stages. To my knowledge, no such remedy is written or spoken of anywhere else. It is:

"Three pinches Rosemary; two pinches dill; one spoonful of crush lavender. Boil in one cup of water with black licorice for one hour, at a high boil. Leave it to cool overnight, then force the vampire in question to drink it in its entirety. Of course, this is useless without the ceremony that accompanies it. One must chant the ancient Latin script, used by the church used for thousands of years—"

Caitlin's heart stopped. As she turned the page, she saw that the next page in the book, the one with the ceremony on it, was torn in half. She could not believe it. Half of the page sat loose in the book, between the pages, displaying only part of the Latin ceremony. The other half of the page was missing.

Caitlin turned all of the pages in the book frantically; she hung the book hung upside down, shaking it. But, to her dismay, the other half was just not there.

No, she thought. *Not now. Not when she was this close. It wasn't fair.*

Caitlin sat there, her heart pounding, wondering what to do. She immediately pulled out her keyboard, went online, typed in the name of the volume, and searched for any other copies of it.

Of course, there were none. It said this was a rare book, on loan, from England. As she searched the internet, it confirmed her worst fears: this was the only copy of the book in existence.

How could it be? Why was the page torn in half? Who had torn it? When? And why? Was it centuries ago? Was it a vampire, or some dark force, that didn't want this ritual to get out?

Caitlin felt struck with the urgency of time. The ritual only worked before the vampire's first kill. Had Scarlet killed anyone yet? How much time did Caitlin have before she did? Was it already too late?

Caitlin extracted the loose, torn page from the book, and held it in her hands. She stared at it, knowing that she couldn't let this go. She had to find the other half. She felt guilty, holding it there like that, with both her hands, out in the open, when every instinct in her, a rare book scholar, told her that the page should be protected, inserted back into the book it came from. But she couldn't help it. Scarlet's life was at stake here.

As she held the page, she realized she could not let it go. She had to steal this page, take it with her, out of the library, and then do whatever she could to find the other half.

"Caitlin?" came a voice.

Caitlin jumped in her chair, quickly hiding the page, and spun around. Over her stood Mrs. Gardiner, the old woman who oversaw the library, short, with gray puffy hair and glasses. She looked down at her, expressionless, as she held a bunch of books in her arm.

"I didn't know you had come in today," she said, disapprovingly.

As Caitlin looked up at her, she could have sworn she saw her glancing at the books on her desk, at all the titles—and even, possibly, at the loose page on her desk. Her heart pounded. She felt like a criminal.

"Um...yes...I...um...came in early," she said, thinking quickly. "I wanted to catch up on work."

Mrs. Gardiner was definitely looking at the titles on her desk, and she saw her eyes widen in surprise.

"Is that one of our display window titles?" she asked, surprised.

Caitlin quickly turned and picked up the book, flustered, not knowing what to say. She had to think quick.

"Um...yes it is," she said. "There were some occult titles I had to catalog, and I...um...wanted context in knowing how best to classify them...so I thought I'd take a look at everything we had on the subject."

It was a lame excuse, and she hoped Mrs. Gardiner bought it.

Mrs. Gardiner stood there, pausing for a moment, and Caitlin felt a cold sweat break out on the back of her neck. She had never been in this position before, feeling like a criminal. Of course, she'd never thought about stealing a book, not in her entire career.

"Well, I trust you will put it all back when you're through," Ms. Gardner said, then nodded curtly and walked on.

Caitlin breathed a sigh of relief. It was a close call.

Caitlin turned, grabbed the loose page from her desk, looked both ways, and made sure no one was looking. She looked up at the ceiling, at the hidden cameras. She knew she was being recorded, so she conspicuously put the loose page back in the book she found it in.

She walked the book down the hall, back towards the stack, went to a place where she knew there was a blind spot from the cameras, then quickly slipped the page out of the book and into a manila folder she had brought with her. She then put the book away, and slid the manila folder into her bag.

Without waiting another second, Caitlin marched down the corridor, down the sleek-white steps, and across the lobby. She looked straight ahead as she went for the front doors, not daring to look at her colleagues, her heart pounding as she felt like she was walking out of a bank with a rare jewel.

She stepped outside with a breath of relief. She hurried to her car, and sat there, breathing deeply. She thought about her next move. She knew who she needed to talk to. Aiden. If there was anyone in the world who would know where to find the missing page, it would be him.

But she still couldn't bring herself to call him. She thought again of his words, of stopping Scarlet, and something inside her would not allow her to speak to him.

Instead, she had an idea. If vampires were real, if her journal was real, then all those places she mentioned in her journal had to be real, too. And some of those were in New York. Like the Cloisters. If everything she had written was true, then she should find something there, some evidence, some validation, some trace of her being there. Some trace that vampires had existed. Maybe even a clue, or a lead. Maybe it would even show her where to go next.

Without another thought, Caitlin tore out of the parking lot, heading for New York City. She was determined not to return home until she found the proof she needed.

CHAPTER FOURTEEN

Scarlet walked with Blake and his three buddies, Vivian and her two friends, across the acres of fields belonging to their high school. She trailed behind. The small group was heading down to the woods, and as they walked, all laughing, jostling each other, as if the closest of friends, Scarlet couldn't help but feel left out. She was beginning to think this was a bad idea.

Vivian clutched hard to Blake, practically sticking to him like a magnet as they walked, and her two friends constantly giggled and whispered in her ear, clearly trying to make Scarlet feel left out. Blake's buddies weren't doing much better, jostling amongst themselves, or trying to talk to Vivian's friends.

Blake himself was the biggest disappointment. He walked with Vivian as if *she* were the one he'd invited, allowing her to clutch his arm as if they were boyfriend and girlfriend. Scarlet was confused. After all, Blake had asked *her* to go. Was he that afraid of upsetting Vivian? Was he too weak to resist her? Or was he genuinely changing his mind, and starting to have feelings for Vivian instead?

Scarlet's apprehension grew as the reality sank in of her cutting class, missing her last two classes of the day—and an important quiz—to be with this group. Had she made a mistake? Her entire reason for going was to be with Blake—and he hardly seemed to even care. He only looked back over his shoulder for her once or twice. With every step, Scarlet felt increasingly left out. But it was too late to turn back now: they were far from school, and had already entered a trail in the woods, which she was unfamiliar with. She followed them as they twisted and turned down the narrow path, feeling increasingly dependent on them to get back.

Finally, the trail ended and led out to the edge of a small, blue lake. Beautiful trees surrounded the water, and their foliage was strewn all around the shore, bright leaves floating in the water. The sight took Scarlet's breath away: it was beautiful down here. She'd been here once before, and remembered it as a favorite place for kids to escape to on weekends. She had never been down here during a school day, though, and it was weird now, quiet and empty. It felt wrong to be here. She felt she should be back in class.

The group found a spot on the shore, close to the water, and they all took makeshift seats on various logs, stumps, and boulders. They sat in a loose circle. Scarlet went to sit beside Blake, but Vivian directed him to a small log, just big enough to hold the two of them, and Scarlet had to sit on the other side of him, on a rock, a few feet away. Blake looked over at her, and she could see that he felt a bit guilty. But still, he wasn't doing anything to change it.

A cool breeze swept in off the lake, and Scarlet hugged her green, fall jacket tightly around her chest, starting to feel cold. She felt shaky, but didn't know if it was from the weather, or from feeling so left out, so nervous to be with this crowd who she barely knew. She wondered how she got herself into this mess to begin with. She should have listened to Maria. She shouldn't have come. A part of her just wanted to get up and leave, but she couldn't bring herself to.

One of Blake's friends skimmed rocks along the lake. Another reached into his jacket pocket and started rolling up small pieces of paper.

Scarlet blinked, shocked to see that he was rolling up a joint. Pot. She couldn't believe it. It was Richard, Blake's best friend, also on the football team, short and stocky, with bright blonde hair. She'd always known that he was trouble, but didn't suspect he'd be smoking pot, especially during a school day.

In moments he had a joint rolled and lit; he took a deep hit and then, to Scarlet's dread, he passed it around. Blake's other buddy, another football player, took it and inhaled deeply. He coughed as he did, and Vivian's friends erupted in sharp, mocking laughter. He turned red, embarrassed, but then inhaled again, determined, and managed to hold it this time.

He passed it along, continuing around the circle, counter-clockwise.

Scarlet's heart started to pound as she realized the joint was being passed around and would head her way. Everyone else was inhaling it. She was the last person in the circle, and knew that it would come her way—and that Blake would be the one to hand it to her.

She felt more disappointed than ever. She hated peer pressure, had never smoked pot before, and didn't intend on starting now. Sure, a few times she had sipped some beers or wine coolers at a party. But that was about it. That was where she drew the line.

But as everyone passed it around the circle, she felt more and more pressure. If she was the only one to say no, she would be so conspicuous, would look like a goody-goody. Which she didn't want to look like in front of Blake. She was torn.

The joint reached Vivian, who sucked on it for an extra-long time, filling her lungs. She then turned, grabbed Blake by the back of his head, leaned in, put her lips on his, and blew into his mouth.

The small group oohed and ahhed as she did.

Blake was clearly surprised, caught off guard. But again, he didn't try to pull away. He let her do it, inhaled, then coughed it out.

Scarlet watched in shock and disgust. She had never guessed Vivian would be that aggressive—and she had never guessed Blake would be that cruel, to allow her to kiss him like that, right in front of her. She felt more snubbed than ever.

As Blake reached over and held out the joint to her, Scarlet just sat there, staring at it, in shock. She hardly knew what to do. Either Blake was really into Vivian, or he didn't have the guts to show it to everyone. Including himself.

For the first time, Scarlet stopped wanting Blake. She just didn't care anymore. For the first time, she realized she was better than all this. She didn't need to take this kind of treatment from him.

"What's the matter—you chicken?" mocked one of Vivian's friends.

"Bac-bac-bac-bac-bac!" another one of Vivian's friends said, making chicken noises.

Scarlet had enough. She rose, turned, and walked away from the group, heading back towards the forest.

"Goody-goody!" screamed one of Blake's buddies.

"Loser!" screamed one of Vivian's friends.

"Let her go," Vivian yelled out. "She's just a waste of space anyway."

Scarlet felt herself tearing up as she hurried away from the group, back towards the forest trail. She was so mad at herself for agreeing to come.

"Scarlet!" came Blake's voice.

He yelled out after her, and she heard the regret in his voice.

But she didn't care anymore. It was too late.

106

She hurried into the forest trail, breaking into a jog as she ran farther and farther away, wiping tears. Behind her, she heard a rustling of leaves, getting closer. She already sensed who it was: Blake.

"Scarlet, please!" he yelled out.

She could hardly believe it: he had left the group, and was running after her.

Soon he caught up to her, cut her off, and she had no choice but to stop. She was now crying, and she looked down, wiping away her tears, as he stood across from her, holding her shoulder. She turned her head, looking away from him.

"I'm sorry," he said. "I really didn't mean for it to go down like that."

"Why did you leave?" she snapped back. "You like Vivian. It's obvious. Why did you even ask me to come?"

"I don't like her," he answered.

"Then you shouldn't have let her kiss you," she snapped back. "Especially in front of me."

For once, Scarlet was standing up for herself, saying what she felt and believed, and it felt good. She no longer felt afraid to voice her feelings. Even to Blake.

It was Blake's turn to look down. She could see the regret in his face.

"You're right. I shouldn't have. I'm sorry."

"Whatever," she said, looking away. "We're just different people. We're into different things. I'm sorry, but I don't cut school. I don't get high. It's just not me. I think you're better off with her."

"But it's not me either," he pleaded back, his face softening. "It's really not," he continued. "I…I guess…I was just…trying to impress you."

"Impress me?" she asked, dumbfounded.

"Show you how cool I was. Cutting school, smoking, all that. I'm sorry. It was stupid."

She looked at him, and could see his sincerity. It made her wonder. Was he really being sincere? She felt that he was. He had been trying to impress her.

She thought about that, and for the first time it dawned on her: that meant he liked her. He really liked her. Her. Scarlet. Not Vivian.

"Can we start over?" he asked. "Just you and me?"

She stared at him, debating. A fall breeze blew up a bunch of leaves by their feet, and he reached out for her hand.

"I know a great spot. Down by the river. Just the two of us. Without my friends. And without Vivian. You're the one I want to be with. Please. Can I try again?"

He was smiling.

Slowly, she broke into a smile, too. She couldn't help it. This time, it felt right.

She reached out and took his hand, and it fit perfectly in hers.

They headed off down the trail, sloping towards the river. He clasped her fingers between his, and she found herself clasping his back.

Despite herself, she found herself hopeful once again.

*

Scarlet and Blake walked through the forest trail, thick with leaves, down the gentle slope, heading through the trails towards the river. As they went, the wind picked up, blowing scores of leaves off the trees. They showered down all around them and as they hit the late afternoon sun, all the different colors lit up brilliantly. It was magical.

Blake held her hand the entire time, and Scarlet felt as if she were walking into a fantasy, a fairy tale. She felt her heart warm with each step, felt herself filling with newfound feelings for Blake, with hope for their relationship. She was feeling good about them again, just as she had that night they went to the movie. Vivian was slowly becoming a distant memory.

Scarlet smiled to herself, as she thought of what her reaction must be right now, sitting around the lake with her friends and Blake's friends, probably waiting for Blake to come back. It probably really peeved her to see him run off after Scarlet.

Finally, Scarlet thought. *A small victory.*

Deep down, though, Scarlet knew that Vivian, being as vindictive and spiteful as she was, would not let this go so easily. She felt sure she would make it her life's mission to slander Scarlet, to turn the school against her. She'd probably wage a malicious gossip campaign, and do who knows what to get back at her. After all, Scarlet had embarrassed her in front of her friends.

Scarlet forced herself to snap out of it. Now wasn't the time to think of Vivian, or of any stress that might come later. Now was the time to live in the moment, to enjoy her time with Blake. Finally, she had what she wanted.

"I know a great spot," Blake said, reading her mind just as she started to wonder where at the riverbank they were going. It broke the long silence between them. "I think you'll really like it."

Scarlet sensed that she would. The further they walked, the more she felt it was just the two of them, the last ones left in the world, leaving everything, all their worries, behind. School, teachers, homework, friends, parents…it all faded with every step they took.

The trees opened up, and Scarlet stood there and paused, amazed by the view. They were at the top of a small hill, covered in knee-high grass and wildflowers, sparkling in the late afternoon sun. In the distance, just beyond it, was the Hudson River. In all her years here, Scarlet had never seen it look so beautiful as it did from this spot, as she looked down on it, with a sweeping view of the trees on both sides of it, of the mountains on the horizon. Scattered clouds filled the sky, and a slow tugboat made its way down the middle of the immense river. She felt as if she'd stepped into a postcard.

Blake tugged on her hand, and they continued down a small, worn path through the flowers, under the open sky, heading closer to the shore. They reached a set of train tracks, about twenty feet away from the river. She stopped, looking both ways, then down at the rails.

"It's okay," Blake said. "Trust me."

He took her hand and led her onto the tracks. They looked quickly in both directions, saw no train anywhere in sight, then sprinted across them, running down the other slope. Scarlet could feel her heart racing and they laughed as they went. In another twenty yards they found themselves at the water's edge.

There was a small, rocky shore, the waves of the Hudson splashing against it, filled with driftwood, glass bottles, and small piles of burnt logs, remnants of a bonfire. Scarlet walked to the water's edge, reached down, and felt the waves with her palm. The water was ice cold, as she expected it to be at the end of October. Still, it was refreshing to the touch.

Blake wandered away from her, and for a moment, she wondered where he was going. He stopped at the water's edge and squatted down, combing the sand with his hand fingers as if looking for something. He was looking beneath the water, every time the tide receded, until finally he found whatever it was he was searching for.

He stood and smiled at her, revealing his perfect teeth, his eyes gleaming in the light. It was a smile that completed her world. He was beaming, and Scarlet could see how genuinely happy and relaxed he was. Happy to be with her, she realized. The thought of it made her feel good.

"Close your eyes," he said softly. "I have a surprise."

Scarlet smiled as she closed her eyes. She could hear Blake approaching, his footsteps crunching the rocks and driftwood.

"Hold out your hand," he said.

She opened her palm, waiting, curious.

After a moment, he placed something cold and damp in her palm. She opened her eyes and looked.

She gasped. He'd inserted into her hand the most beautiful piece of sea glass she had ever seen, completely smooth, worn by the waves of the Hudson. It was a vibrant rose color, and seemed to glow in the fading sun.

Sea glass. Somehow, it felt meaningful to Scarlet, like it brought back memories. Although of what, she didn't know.

Before she could thank him, he'd already taken her hand and was leading her down the shore.

"This way," he said.

They twisted and turned along the shoreline, down a narrow path, weaving in and out of the tall marsh. After a few minutes, they turned a bend, and Scarlet was amazed at what lay before them: there sat a small grove of trees, clustered at the shore, their branches leaning over the river. Fruit hung from the branches.

Apples. She couldn't believe it. An apple orchard, here, in all places, right up against the water.

"The best picking in town," Blake said with a smile, as he turned to her. "No one else knows about it. They just grow wild and fall into the water. Might as well enjoy it, right?"

Smiling, he took her hand and led her to the first tree. The trees were small, only about twelve feet high, with old, wide branches arching low to the ground. Blake easily stepped up onto one of the branches, then another, and took a seat on a wide branch. He turned and held out a hand for Scarlet.

It looked like fun, and she loved climbing trees.

110

"I got it," she said with a smile, and quickly and easily climbed up the branches, until she was sitting beside him.

He looked back at her, impressed by her dexterity.

She reached up and picked a huge, green apple hanging over her head. She had to yank hard to get it off, and as she did, a cluster of apples came falling off their branches, a mini avalanche bouncing all around them. She raised her hand to her head, as one bounced off it. Several landed in the water, bobbing, immediately carried away by the strong tides of the Hudson.

She turned to Blake, in shock, and he looked back at her, equally shocked. At the same time, they both burst into laughter.

"I think you just discovered gravity," he joked.

They laughed together, as Scarlet watched the apples drift further and further out into the Hudson. As she watched, a large fish suddenly surfaced and took a bite out of one of them.

"Oh my God, did you see that?" she said excitedly, pointing.

Another fish came up and took a bite out of another one. They laughed in amazement.

Blake turned back to the tree, reaching up and carefully picking an apple himself. Scarlet bit into hers. It was the biggest apple she'd ever had, the size of a grapefruit, and the most crisp, too. It was delicious, and she realized how hungry she was. In no time, she ate nearly half the apple, its juice running down her chin.

She suddenly felt self-conscious, wiping her chin with the back of her hand.

"Sorry," she said, her mouth full.

"For what?" Blake asked, his own mouth full, and with twice as much juice dripping down his chin.

They both laughed.

They finished their apples and both sat there, looking out at the sunset, watching the fading sun over the river.

After a while, strong breezes picked up, whistling through, and she began to feel cold. She was trembling, and buttoned the highest button of her jacket.

Blake reached out and draped an arm around her shoulder.

As he did, Scarlet's heart started to beat faster. She had never been touched by Blake before, not like that, and the feel of it was electrifying. She was scared; yet she didn't want him to back away.

She leaned slightly into him, and he kept his arm around her shoulder, pulling her close to him. They sat side-by-side, their shoulders touching. He slowly ran his hand up and down her arm, warming her.

Then he reached out with his other hand, and laid it gently on top of hers.

"My God, you're freezing," he said.

Scarlet quickly retracted her hand, self-conscious. She'd also noticed recently that her hands seemed colder than usual.

"Sorry," she said.

"It doesn't bother me," he said. "Your hands—they're beautiful."

Blake reached down, and slowly pulled her hand back, and held it in his.

Her heart was pounding as he slowly caressed her hand. She was trembling again, but this time it wasn't from the cold. It was from nervousness. She felt sure he was about to kiss her. A part of her wanted him to. But another part still wasn't sure.

Her heart pounded in her throat as Blake slowly turned from the river, facing her. She turned her chin just the slightest bit towards his, to see if he was looking at her.

She could see out of the corner of her eye that he was, and she turned to him a bit more.

That was all he needed. He reached up with his free hand and held her cheek in his palm. She turned more to him, and for a moment, they looked deeply into each other's eyes.

He leaned in, and a moment later, she felt his soft lips on hers. It was a gentle kiss, and her heart was pounding as their lips met.

The kiss lasted for an eternity.

As she closed her eyes, she felt transported to another world.

She kissed him back. He reached up and ran his hand through her hair, then slowly across her neck. She leaned in a bit more, and they kissed more passionately.

Suddenly, something began to rise up within her. It was a feeling, something she did not recognize. Her heart suddenly started to slam, to pound out of her chest. It felt like she was having a heart attack. Then she felt an intense heat, a burning, rising up her legs, through her torso, down her arms, to her fingertips. She felt an awful stab of hunger, of pain, deep in her solar plexus. For a moment, it felt as if she'd been stabbed. It took her breath away.

She did not understand what was happening to her. She thought maybe she was dying.

And then she found herself staring right at Blake's neck. She zoomed in, watched the tiny heartbeat pulsing in his veins. His scent filled every pore of her body. She felt an unquenchable desire to be close to him.

But not to kiss him. To her own horror, she found her body screaming at her, begging her, to sink her teeth into his neck. To feed on him. To drink his blood.

Suddenly, she felt her two incisor teeth begin to expand. To grow. To sharpen.

Immediately, she pulled back, closing her mouth, looking away.

"What is it?" he asked, surprised. "What's wrong?"

But she couldn't sit there another second. Her body was screaming at her to do something that her mind couldn't understand. What was happening?

She didn't know. But she did know that she couldn't risk being around Blake for one more second. She knew that if she looked at him again, if she turned his way, for a fraction of a second, it would be over. She would be unable to control herself.

So without another word she leapt down off the tree, and sprinted away, bounding across the tracks, up the hill, back towards the forest trail. She ran with a speed and agility she never knew she had—and within just a few seconds, was far, far away from the river. From Blake.

And far from the Scarlet she once knew.

Now Available!

CRAVED:
Book #2 of the Vampire Legacy

In CRAVED (Book #2 of the Vampire Legacy series), 16 year old Scarlet Paine struggles to find out exactly what she's becoming. Her erratic behavior has alienated her new boyfriend, Blake, and she struggles to make amends, and to make him understand. But the problem is, she doesn't understand herself what's happening to her.

At the same time, the new boy, the mysterious Sage, comes into her life. Their paths keep intertwining, and although she tries to avoid it, he directly pursues her, despite the objections of her best friend, Maria, who's convinced Scarlet is stealing Sage. Scarlet finds herself swept away by Sage, who takes her into his world, past the gates of his family's historic river mansion. As their relationship deepens, she begins to learn more about his mysterious past, his family, and the secrets he must hold. They spend the most romantic time she can imagine, on a secluded island in the Hudson, and she is convinced she has found the true love of her life.

But then she is devastated to learn Sage's biggest secret of all: he is not human, either, and he has only a few weeks left to live. Tragically, just at the moment when destiny has brought her greatest love, it also seems fated to take him away.

As Scarlet returns to the high school parties leading up to the big dance, she ends up in a huge falling-out with her friends, who excommunicate her from their group. At the same time, Vivian rounds up the popular girls to make her life hell, leading to an unavoidable confrontation. Scarlet's forced to sneak out, making matters worse with her parents, and soon finds pressure building from all sides. The only light in her life is Sage. But he is still holding back some of his secrets, and Blake resurfaces, determined to pursue her.

Caitlin, meanwhile, is determined to find a way to reverse Scarlet's vampirism. What she discovers leads her on a journey to find the antidote, deep into the heart of rare libraries and bookstores, and she will stop at nothing until she has it.

But it may be too late. Scarlet is changing rapidly, barely able to control what she's becoming. She wants to end up with Sage—but fate seems set on tearing them apart. As the book culminates in an action-packed and shocking twist, Scarlet will be left with a monumental choice—one that will change the world forever. How much is she willing to risk for love?

Books by Morgan Rice

THE SORCERER'S RING
A QUEST OF HEROES (BOOK #1)
A MARCH OF KINGS (BOOK #2)
A FEAST OF DRAGONS (BOOK #3)
A CLASH OF HONOR (BOOK #4)
A VOW OF GLORY (BOOK #5)
A CHARGE OF VALOR (BOOK #6)
A RITE OF SWORDS (BOOK #7)
A GRANT OF ARMS (BOOK #8)
A SKY OF SPELLS (BOOK #9)
A SEA OF SHIELDS (BOOK #10)
A REIGN OF STEEL (BOOK #11)

THE SURVIVAL TRILOGY
ARENA ONE (Book #1)
ARENA TWO (Book #2)

the Vampire Journals
turned (book #1)
loved (book #2)
betrayed (book #3)
destined (book #4)
desired (book #5)
betrothed (book #6)
vowed (book #7)
found (book #8)
resurrected (book #9)
craved (book #10)